Lessons in Seduction

Melissa Schroeder

A Samhain Publishing, Ltd. publication.

Samhain Publishing, Ltd.
512 Forest Lake Drive
Warner Robins, GA 31093
www.samhainpublishing.com

Lessons in Seduction
Copyright © 2007 by Melissa Schroeder
Print ISBN: 1-59998-560-8
Digital ISBN: 1-59998-610-8

Editing by Sasha Knight
Cover by Scott Carpenter

First Samhain Publishing, Ltd. electronic publication: October 2007
First Samhain Publishing, Ltd. print publication: January 2008

Dedication

To my daughters. Thanks for putting up with endless late dinners, mood swings, lack of any kind of domestic abilities outside of cooking, the endless string of deadlines I am working to meet and my inability to remember what day of the week it is. Thank you for your love and support, and for our girls' nights. Remember, Mommy will always love you just the way you are, even though you look like the stinky boy we share the house with.

Love,

Mommy

Chapter One

In which Lady Cicely formulates a plan.

When a woman reaches the age of six and twenty, thought Cicely Ware with a matter-of-factness that would frighten the majority of the ton, she had to face the truth about her future. In her humble opinion, it showed an amazing fortitude and an abundance of maturity to contemplate what her future held for her. Unfortunately, with one as apparently bleak as hers, facing it was not a pleasant experience.

With interest, she watched the expert moves of the couples as they danced a country reel. The ladies' beautifully ornate skirts floated about their ankles as the soft candlelight cast a golden shimmer on the magnificent surroundings. Even in the elegant setting and in the presence of some of the most attractive people in London, depression threatened to dim Cicely's spirits. That troubled her. She had never been one to allow her emotions to consume or control her. Now it was different. This melancholy had been happening with greater frequency lately. It was her damned common sense that kept doing her in. Reality wasn't something from which she shied, not with all her negative family history in these recent years.

She sighed, hating the fact she was so practical. Her life would be so much easier if she were a scatterbrain. If she gave a fig about her appearance—which only depressed her further—her life would be simpler. She could spend her time wrapped up in fabrics and designs. She would know what the latest was, and care. She could pour herself into wasting inordinate amounts of other people's money on gowns and accoutrements that would be worn only once. Even the thought made her queasy. Maybe if she did those things...

If she could but smile and laugh when a man said stupid things. If she could look the other way at indiscretion. If she could whittle away the hours with embroidery or nonsense. If she could forget her worries, her family, her life... There had been that one glimmer of hope. That the dowry Sebastian provided might bring an offer of marriage.

Cicely snorted and received a look of remonstration from an elderly spinster seated to her right. Immediately, she pulled her features back into the placid expression of a soon-to-be spinster happy with her lot in life. If she must sit with them, she had to blend into the crowd. People wanted her there. They wanted her body in attendance, not her mind. They didn't care about her feelings or desires. So it wouldn't do to let others see that what she yearned for most was to marry and have children. It upset members of the ton, not to mention the other unwed women, to know that she was not truly and wonderfully happy alone. She had no idea why it was any of their business. As long as she kept her mouth shut, normally she was fine. The slip of the face had been a mistake. For some reason, the aristocracy couldn't handle anyone being sad at a ball.

She wasn't sad, actually. Disappointed would be a better word. No one knew this about her. She didn't have close friends in which she could confide. There was no one to tell her innermost secrets to. More than anything she wanted to find a man to love, to have children to raise. Simple pleasures of life. But at six and twenty, she knew the truth. That was never going to happen. The last few years had been a strain. Now that the rumors about her family had reached polite society, hope of a match had dimmed. Suitable or otherwise. No matter how well the family hid the truth, part of it, the nastiest parts, had seeped out. Rumors that her mother was mad and had tried to kill her cousin, and that her father had died of an apoplexy in a whore's bed, tended to discourage even the most ardent admirer, let alone a man considering marrying her for no other reason than her money. Not to mention the slight detail that she had shot her own mother. That tended to put a man off.

People still whispered. It would be wrong to talk openly about her and her pitiful situation. The whispers wounded her more deeply than she cared to admit. But the loneliness was what pained her the most.

She would never wed. She would never know the joy of having her own children reach for her hand or call her mama. And she would never fall in love. She would never be held in the adoring embrace of a man who saw her as his one and only. Love was complicated, and it hurt. She had seen it when Sebastian's first wife had cheated on him, and she saw it within many marriages among the ton.

Each season, some misguided fool married for what she believed was love, only to find herself married to a man who only cared about her dowry. Her cousin, Sebastian, and his wife, Colleen, loved each other. Cicely knew without a doubt how special their match was. But they were an oddity. She would never be able to snag a man's attention enough to make him fall in love and there was nothing sadder than a woman pining after a man who kept a string of mistresses.

Oh, she didn't think she was ugly. People didn't hide their children from her in fear, but she was plain. Freckles, boring brown eyes and straight brown hair, and a penchant for reading history didn't make her the catch of the season. That much, she was sure of. She lacked the ability to attract men. The gallant flocked to the stunning. The scholarly to the brilliant. The rich to the rich. The few men she was close to tended to view her as a little sister.

She had always thought if her mother had not pushed her on the marriage mart all those years ago, she might have had a chance. There had been several local families near their Hampshire property with bookish types of sons. They would have been perfect for her. Those men would not care if she wasn't dressed in the latest fashions, if she wasn't an Incomparable. Men in London did.

After two years of hoping that the large dowry would help, Cicely had decided she needed a better plan. She confronted the truth of her spinsterhood with a brave face, turned-up, freckled nose included, and accepted that she may never marry, but she would not die a virgin.

As soon as the thought of her plan popped into her head, her face flushed with heat. She glanced around. Even though she had kept her thoughts private, she could not help but feel as if the whole world could hear them.

When no one appeared to notice, she relaxed. Silly, really, to think that someone would know what she was thinking. Most people probably thought she was contemplating her next meeting of The Historical Society or perhaps her next visit to the book loan. That is if they cared to wonder at her thoughts at all. Shaking away the worry, she thought about her plan. It was a brilliant notion, if she did say so herself. She'd turned the idea over in her mind for weeks, weighing the possibilities, and decided it was worth the chance. At first, she had worried that she wouldn't be able to find a suitable candidate. But, she had come to the conclusion that would not be a problem. Men who would hesitate to marry her would not think anything of bedding her.

The next problem arose when she made her list of men. She didn't want a man who didn't know what he was about because she surely didn't know anything, and this would be her one chance to experience physical intimacies with a man. If she approached a buffoon, her only experience would be a disappointment. She'd had too many of those in her life to deal with one more. This was her chance to live and she desired to live well.

Restless, she stood and moved away from the darkened corner and out to the fringes of the milling crowd. Laughter and glasses chimed as the candlelight twinkled. Women and men spun around the dance floor. Others gathered, chatting amicably. They were not the focus of Cicely's inspection. It was the men. There were rakes aplenty in the ton. Most of the unmarried men, and some of the married, had horrible reputations. She allowed herself a brief nod of confirmation. A man who'd perfected the art of seduction and had no qualms about deflowering her was just what she needed. Though, she had decided that she should concentrate on bachelors to begin with. She didn't know if she could take the guilt of being intimate with a man with a wife at home.

The Earl of Dewhurst walked by. Just a couple years older than she, Dewhurst was an attractive gentleman, with chocolate brown eyes and a kind smile, complete with a dimple. He was on her list, although he had not ranked in the top five. She noticed a few more of her candidates loitering about the room, including Bridgerton. But he was at the bottom of her list. Not for lack of quality, but rather for the fact he would undoubtedly tell Sebastian in an instant.

Another sigh escaped before she could stop it.

You really must learn control, she reprimanded herself.

Sebastian used to be fun, until he'd taken over as head of the family. Now he took his duties seriously. Not a week went by when he didn't lecture his sister Anna on her behavior. Cicely was quite put out that he didn't feel the need to lecture her. It was as if he was sure of her conduct. However... She pursed her lips. This could work in her favor. Sebastian would probably doubt Bridgerton if he claimed she'd propositioned him. Perhaps she could add him back to the prey...perhaps even move him up the list. She had other candidates if he should decline. It was such a bother having a boring reputation.

She shook her head. No. Bridgerton was a last resort.

There was also the problem of finding a man who made her insides turn to mush and her skin tingle. Bridgerton didn't actually do that, but he was well known for his skills in the bedroom.

No. She had another man in mind. Every time she saw him, her brain went blank. She knew he would be perfect, if only he would agree with her plan. Ahhh. A murmur of feminine whispers rose above the music, signaling his arrival. Whispering and giggling always rose to an irritating volume when he entered the room. It was as inevitable as William the Great's success in 1066.

She slowly turned in the direction of the entrance, her heart pounding, her body warming just at the thought he was there. Then, she saw him.

Douglas, Duke of Ethingham, was every matchmaking mama's dream come true and nightmare rolled into one delectable package. Cicely had always thought him attractive, although she'd only observed him from a comfortable distance. Since the familial connection between he and Colleen had been revealed, he'd become a regular fixture at the Penwyth townhouse and estate. Cicely and he had become acquaintances of a sort. He rescued her from being a wallflower. She saved him from debutantes and mamas.

She watched him walk through the crowded ballroom, the candlelight caressing his sculpted facial features. From where she stood, his eyes looked ordinary grey. But, she knew about the hint of blue around the iris of his eye and the way it lightened even more when he laughed. Her heart skipped a beat as he headed in her direction.

"You would think he would have been caught by someone by now."

Cicely jumped, startled by the familiar faint whisper in her right ear, then looked over her shoulder at her aunt Victoria. Petite, yet rounded, Victoria was still the beauty she had been in her youth. While fine lines around most ladies' eyes would make them appear older, it just added character to Victoria's face.

They were much the same height, yet Cicely always felt like an elephant next to her. She turned back around but realized she'd lost sight of Douglas. Disappointed, she gave her attention back to her aunt, an empty feeling lining her gut. He had seen her. She knew it. But, he'd seen something better. She tried to push the negative thoughts from her mind and focus on her aunt.

"I have a feeling that His Grace will not be caught unless he wants to be caught."

Victoria laughed and stepped forward to stand beside Cicely. "That much we agree. Still, he is getting to the point where he should think about putting up a nursery. He is the end of his line. Well, the only one worth anything anyway. I know there is a cousin or two somewhere, but rumor is they are as ghastly as his father and grandfather."

Something cold slithered into Cicely's stomach and settled there. Not from her aunt's description of Douglas' extended family, but rather from the thought of him with another woman. She knew he had to marry, though she had hoped it would not be so soon. At least not until after he helped her with her plan. Okay, really never. If he did have to wed, sharing one memorable night with him would be enough for her to endure whatever simpering fool he married.

She cleared her throat delicately. "His Grace has said before he does not intend to marry for some time."

When Victoria didn't respond, Cicely glanced at her. A mysterious smile played about her aunt's lips.

"You know what they say, Cicely. The right woman could make any man change his mind."

She doubted any woman would change the duke's mind, but she nodded just to agree and get the conversation moving. Knowing that this would probably disintegrate into another discussion on her lack of beaus, something that apparently confused her aunt, Cicely decided to change the subject.

"Did I tell you about the diary I found today at the bookstore?"

Victoria gave her a knowing look but said nothing about her lack of tact. "No, you didn't."

"It was quite amazing I found it because it was buried at the bottom of a crate. The proprietor told me he'd bought it at some estate sale."

"Really?" Victoria's attention had now turned back to the dancers on the floor, but Cicely knew that her aunt had a habit of keeping one eye on her surroundings and her ear to the conversation.

"It is more an accounting than a personal diary. I am not sure what it means or if it is real. But it seems that one of five men kept a diary while they conspired against the throne about the time of the Terror. I have no idea from where they came, but I think they may be very significant."

The first strains of a waltz sounded before Victoria could answer. Cicely really hated this dance. While she sometimes had requests for country dances from various cousins and gentlemen she knew from The Historical Society, she rarely was asked to waltz.

"Lady Cicely."

She glanced over her shoulder to find Douglas standing to her left, a smile curving his beautiful lips. Curling her toes into her slippers, she told her heart to stop doing flip-flops. All she could do was stare at him. His wavy dark hair never seemed to stay in place, yet always looked tidy. The mischievous twinkle in his eye sent heat racing up her spine. A few murmurs reached her and brought her out of her stupor. It was then she realized her faux pas. Flushing, she curtsied.

"Your Grace."

He took her offered hand and waited for her to rise before asking, "Would you honor me with this dance?"

She didn't pretend not to hear the whispers growing louder. Accustomed to them or not, they were still disturbing. Regardless, she held her head high and looked him right in the eye. "I would be delighted to dance with you, Your Grace."

He led her out to the dance floor and within moments they were whirling with the other dancers. The feel of his strong hand providing gentle pressure on her waist, his body close to hers made her head spin. The heat of him warmed her front, though she tried not to think about it. Her body already tingled, and she knew from experience she lost all thought when that happened.

"I owe you a world of thanks, Lady Cicely." He smiled down at her, a genuine smile because the man thought she was no threat to his bachelorhood. And she wasn't. She didn't want marriage, but she did want him. "Lady Sara has been after me since I walked in the door and I shudder to think what would happen if I had to dance with her."

She tried not to laugh, but she couldn't help it. "You should be ashamed of yourself, Your Grace. She cannot help it that she can't dance."

"I danced with her last week and my feet will never be the same. Who would have thought such a small woman could inflict that much pain?" He shook his head and chuckled, clearly amused with himself. "So I am serious when I tell you I owe you a boon."

This was almost too good to be true. "You will grant me a favor in return?"

He nodded and expertly twirled them around a slower couple. She licked her lips and numbly followed his lead. Truthfully, she knew he thought nothing of the offer. In Douglas' mind, she was sure he assumed she might ask for a ride in the park, or the use of his box at the theater. This had been handed to her on her silver dancing card.

"Your Grace?"

He leaned closer to hear her. She normally didn't speak that loud, but with the sound of the orchestra, not to mention the fact she was out of breath from dancing, she understood he was having problems hearing her.

"I call in your boon. I do have a favor to ask of you."

Nodding, he straightened and again twirled her around. "Ask and you shall receive."

"I was wondering, if you wouldn't mind, would you teach me how to seduce a man?"

Douglas, Duke of Ethingham, stopped in mid-step and stared down at Lady Cicely completely nonplussed. Never in his life did he expect that to be the favor she asked him.

"What did you say?"

She frowned at him, a little wrinkle appearing between her finely sculpted brows. A couple ran into his back, causing him to trip forward, his body brushing against Cicely's. For that instant, her breasts, amazing breasts he'd had no idea she had, pressed against his chest, and it knocked the wind out of him. In his arms he felt a woman, lush in all the right places. He shook his head and stepped away, bumping into a dancing couple. Douglas turned and said with a growl, "Would you mind watching where you are going?"

The Earl of Trent and his partner laughed. Trent said, "If you want to hold a discussion, Your Grace, I suggest you leave the dance floor."

"Your Grace? Do you mind?" Cicely asked. Embarrassment and reprimand colored her voice.

The nerve of the chit. She was looking up at him with those velvet brown eyes, and a little pout forming on her full mouth— not that he had ever noticed that either, until now. He pulled her back into his arms and started to waltz again. The steps were automatic. He didn't hear the music. He no longer noticed his surroundings. She demanded his attention—her and her damned question. He forced his grip to gentle and his expression back to bland, which was not easy to do with his heart beating the way it was—or the rush of blood to his groin. Something he had never experienced in her presence before now.

"You needn't look so appalled, Your Grace."

So he had not succeeded with his card face. "I'm not appalled."

She laughed. He realized he hadn't heard her laugh that carefree before this night. The sweet sound captured him and almost had him stopping again on the floor. "Your Grace, I know better than that. The expression on your face was beyond priceless. Do not worry, you have schooled it well."

Another bubble of laughter rose from her throat. Douglas knew he should be mad at her amusement at his expense but he couldn't. In the time he'd known the young woman, he'd not often seen her smile, let alone laugh. He was pleased to see that she seemed to be moving on from her past. And her pleasure was the reason for the delight that wound through him, curling into his heart.

But if he let her know how it had affected him she'd use it to her advantage. It was what women did. Retreating into his role of duke, he said, "Lady Cicely, I doubt very much that Lady Victoria would approve of your suggestion."

She didn't laugh, but she did smile. "I think at my age I can make my own decisions about this. But, since you appear to be so appalled by the idea—"

"I didn't say I was appalled."

She continued as if he hadn't said a word. "Then I shall mark you off my list."

The music drew to a close when she made that comment. They stopped and he released her from his arms, but noticed they were near the French doors that led to the terrace. He should walk her back to Lady Victoria, but her last statement piqued his interest. Against his better judgment, he took her by her elbow and ushered her out into the night.

The dimly lit area was perfect for liaisons, and he had used it to his advantage more than once before. He knew a corner where they would be left alone. He pulled her along in a not-so-gentlemanly fashion.

Once there, he ushered her into the darkened corner. He backed her up against the wall, stepping close enough that the skirts of her gown brushed his legs. They hadn't been this close when they had been waltzing. There was a hint of lavender in the air. He didn't know if it was from her or the garden behind them. Resisting the urge to lean closer and sniff, he crossed his arms over his chest and gave her his best "I am the duke" stare. Bloody chit just smiled at him.

"Really, Your Grace, it is fine. I completely understand. I am a bit plain and not at all to your normal tastes." She licked her lips nervously and he followed the movement. Aggravation burned a hole in his gut as he realized he was wondering how she would taste.

He shook his head, trying to focus. "What I want to know is what you mean by propositioning me while we are waltzing, and what do you mean by mark me off the list?"

She frowned now. He could almost see the wheels turning in her head. Lady Cicely was reserved, but Douglas had always sensed something just below the surface. He knew there were many times, probably through habit, that she refrained from making any comments on a subject. Her intelligence was not unknown, but he wondered how much of it she did hide.

"It really isn't important now that you took yourself out of the running, Your Grace. You offered a boon, I simply asked for what I needed fulfilled. I understand you not wanting to. So this conversation should be closed."

The calm, rational tone of her voice had him grinding his teeth. "I think I need to know just exactly what you are talking about."

She stepped back and came to an abrupt stop when she hit the wall behind her. Narrowing her eyes, she placed a hand on each hip.

"Since you have declined participation, it isn't any of your business." She noticed something over his shoulder and her eyes widened. He turned to look and saw nothing, but had left just enough room for her to scoot around him and out of the corner. Before he realized what she was about, she'd stepped far enough away that he wouldn't be able to grab her arm without some of the other occupants of the terrace noticing. Without turning around she said, "No worry, Your Grace. I will see myself inside. Thank you for the dance."

So the little minx thought she could get away that easily? Irritation lit through him. He was not used to people ignoring his requests.

Suppressing the urge to shout, he said, "Lady Cicely."

She stopped and glanced back at him, one eyebrow cocked. The fire that flashed in her eyes did nothing to cool his reaction to her.

"I would like to discuss this further."

Sighing, she turned completely around to face him. "Your Grace, I know you are accustomed to throwing out orders and having them followed." She drew closer. At first, he thought she might have been a bit apologetic until they made eye contact. Irritation and anger colored her brown eyes, darkening them. "But, you see, you turned me down, so therefore it is none of your business. I am neither your family nor your charge. And I doubt that your ducal powers would encompass my list. We are through here. Now."

With that pronouncement, she turned on her heel and marched back into the ballroom. At first, he couldn't think. He was too stunned. He'd never in his life had a person refute his command. And Cicely, who nary said boo to him in the two years he had known her, had the nerve to tell him no? Then walk away from him?

He stalked toward the French doors, barely able to keep from growling. As he stepped into the ballroom, a wave of heat swept over him and he tugged at his collar. Damn crowds. Even as the mixture of scented perfumes and body odor reached him, he knew his discomfort was more from the social environment than the actual temperature. Matchmaking mamas and their clinging, simpering daughters bored him to tears. He had come tonight because Lady Victoria had asked him to attend. He could never turn down Colleen's mother-in-law. He had a weakness for pretty women, but it went beyond that. Since the discovery of his relation to Colleen, Lady Victoria had treated him as one of the family. To him, that meant the world.

He spotted her talking to Lady Bridgerton in the corner with the other matrons and decided to seek her out. Normally, he would avoid most of the women in that area. More than one of them had a family member they were trying to foist upon him. He took a deep breath. He could take it.

"Your Grace."

He ground his teeth together when he recognized Bridgerton's voice. Douglas repressed the urge to tell the earl to bugger off. He'd gained Bridgerton as a friend when he was accepted as part of the Penwyth family. Just a few years older than Douglas, Daniel still had the matchmaking mamas after him too. With his title, looks, not to mention his ready wit, he was considered a great catch. The same age as Sebastian, he had taken another path than his happily wedded friend. Daniel seemed as disinclined to marry as Douglas was.

"Bridgerton." Douglas nodded as he completely turned to face him. This had better be short. He was on a mission. "Is there something you need?"

He couldn't stop from clenching his teeth. Aggravated didn't begin to describe what he was feeling. His friend's eyebrows rose all the way to his hairline and Douglas silently cursed himself for revealing his feelings. He just could not accept that he had been dismissed, and by a woman who was known for being even-tempered and soft-spoken.

Daniel noticed his state, but didn't comment. "Sebastian wanted me to make sure you came for Jane's baptism tomorrow."

He sighed, thinking of his cousin's newest addition to the family. "I take it that it was my cousin and not Penwyth who asked?"

Daniel's grin grew as did Douglas' irritation. "No. But then, Sebastian lives to make Colleen happy, so I am sure she is behind his request."

Douglas hated family gatherings of any sort. He shifted his weight from foot to foot, trying to quell the uneasiness that had risen. "I told them I would try to make it."

"Not good enough." Daniel grabbed a glass of champagne as a waiter walked by. "Colleen apparently wants you front and center, and you are to ride there with the family. And, before you complain, I have to be there, too."

Sighing, Douglas looked out over the sea of dancers, trying to locate Lady Cicely. When he spotted her, standing in a corner sipping champagne and talking to Dewhurst, panic set in. He didn't have time for this.

"I will be there, what time?" He didn't take his eyes off her as he asked his question. What the devil did she think she was doing with Dewhurst? He was a rake of the first order. When he saw her smile up at the earl, looking through her long lashes, his stomach muscles clenched. Why had he never noticed her smile before tonight? And why was she flirting with Dewhurst? Was he on the blasted list? Whatever that list meant.

Daniel's amused voice broke into his thoughts. "Eleven."

"Eleven what?"

Laughter laced the words, but it had not yet come bursting forth from Daniel's ear-splitting grin. "You asked me what time you were to arrive at the Penwyth townhouse."

"Right. I will see you there."

Without another word, he strode across the ballroom, never taking his eyes off his quarry. He would not allow Lady Cicely to go off making advances on the male population of the ton. Since Sebastian wasn't there, it would have to be he who stepped into the role of guardian and protected the chit. He reassured himself it had nothing to do with his own strange reaction to her this evening. If she were left to her own devices, which apparently she was, she would find herself ruined. He was only trying to save her from herself.

Chapter Two

In which Lady Cicely requests aid from an unlikely source.

The evening had been painfully long and it was not even remotely close to being over. Cicely smiled at the Earl of Dewhurst and wondered, not for the first time in the last few moments, why women were so fascinated with him. He was attractive enough, with his dark brown eyes, strong jaw and ready smile. Dressed always in the first stare of fashion, he certainly cut a fine figure. Debutantes whispered about his prowess, his masculinity. All Cicely could think about was just how boring the man truly was.

Awareness feathered across the back of her neck, as if fingers trailed against her skin. She shivered. She didn't have to turn around to know who approached. As before, her body reacted to the duke's nearness. Her heart pounded even as she silently admonished herself. The man was just not interested. In truth, he had been appalled by the idea of bedding her. She knew that would be a deterrent to any help he might give in that area. If he could not even fathom the deed, how on earth could he help her secure another who might?

It was then that she realized Dewhurst had broken off talking about himself—and wasn't that wonderful—and was gaping at something over her shoulder. She sighed, knowing

Douglas stood there behind her. She didn't like confrontations and she would rather at this point Dewhurst not know about the list and what it was for.

Slowly, trying to appear as if her nerves weren't hopping, she turned to face Douglas. She hoped he couldn't tell how he affected her. Even as she felt a flare of heat warm her cheeks, she met his frank gaze. She would not be pitied again. But what she found shimmering in his grey eyes made her breath catch in her throat. It was not pity she saw there. It was anger. She'd never seen Douglas angry, but there was no mistaking the emotion shadowing his eyes. No wonder Dewhurst had suddenly stopped talking about himself.

"Your Grace." She curtsied. "You know the earl, do you not?" She waved her hand in front of Dewhurst's chest, almost smacking him.

"Yes," Douglas said, his voice cold and hard. "I believe we have met on occasion."

"Y-Y-Your Grace." Dewhurst bowed and when he righted himself, he looked from side to side. He smoothed his richly tailored plum jacket, removing unseen folds and wrinkles. "Ahh, I see my mother has arrived." After excusing himself, he practically ran away.

She watched the earl's retreat with a cross between amusement and astonishment. "Well, Your Grace, you seem to know how to keep the conversation going."

"You're definitely not wasting any time, Lady Cicely."

At first, she couldn't believe he had made reference to their earlier conversation, especially as loudly as he said it. Embarrassment, even though no one knew what he was talking about, and anger intertwined and caused her voice to rise to a level matching his own.

"Your Grace, I was just chatting to Dewhurst about the next Historical Society meeting."

She hoped he didn't realize she was lying. She actually had been talking about that, as Dewhurst did attend some meetings, but he'd had no interest in her discovery. About five minutes into the conversation she had acknowledged the only subject Dewhurst liked to talk about was Dewhurst. Then she'd done no talking. He talked enough for both of them.

"Chatting is a relatively inane name for what you were probably saying to him."

"What makes you think you know what I was saying to him?"

He smiled, but there was no humor in it. "Seeing how you asked me while dancing, I figured you went to the next name on the list."

Of all the nerve! "First of all..." She lowered her voice when she noticed it had risen enough to catch bystanders' attention. "First of all, I asked you then because you said you owed me. That is the only reason I presented the query to you. Second of all, Dewhurst isn't that far up on the list, if you must know. And third of all, it isn't any of your business."

"It is my business. You asked me first. But then, my family connection to you makes it imperative that I watch over you."

Once again, she was knocked speechless. The man had to be one of the most arrogant people on the face of the earth. Granted, he was a duke, but what made him think he could tell her what she could and could not do?

It briefly flitted through her mind to tell him he had not been the first one she had asked, but that was simply petty and it would do no good to lie to him about that. He was angry enough as it was. She tried a different approach. "While I understand your concern, I really don't think there is any need for it. I have changed my mind."

His eyebrows rose slightly, and he studied her. "And what brought about this change?"

Cicely pulled her lower lip between her teeth, trying to think of a lie plausible enough to fool him. She wasn't very good at the whole game of lying. Blushing profusely while telling falsehoods tended to alert people of one's deception. Understanding now just how far his arrogance went, she decided guilt might work. Drawing in a deep breath, she prepared her performance, knowing the threat of tears worked on most men. She'd seen Anna perform this task at least a half dozen times in the last month.

"Truthfully?"

"That would be nice."

"Very well. When you seemed so appalled by the idea, I realized what I was up against." She shook her head dramatically and blinked a few times.

"Lady Cicely—"

"No. No, don't say any more. I completely understand. I do. I see why you would not want me, but please spare me the words. It was foolish to ask you, to even think... Anyway, I wish to put the whole thing behind me." She lowered her head and pitched her voice in such a way that there was no mistaking her horror. If Douglas bought this act, Anna was right. Men were terrified of female tears.

He sighed, and she couldn't help glancing up from beneath her lashes at him. For the first time since Cicely had met him, Douglas not only looked confused, but a tad bit bewildered. She almost felt sorry for him, but she was more worried about diverting his attention. She didn't need another big brother. Certainly not one she thought of with such...adoration.

"Lady Cicely, I apologize for upsetting you."

She looked up, waiting for his next comment, but the bell for dinner rang.

He paused. Cicely watched, amused in spite of her situation. The mixture of emotions that swept over his features ranged from suspicion to irritation to uneasiness. His eyebrows drew down as he narrowed his eyes, studying her as if she were a creature he had never seen before. After a few moments, he released a breath and the tension in his body drained. He may not believe her, but at that moment, he wasn't going to press for information. Holding out his arm, he said, "Would you do me the honor of accompanying me into dinner?"

She smiled at him, relieved he had chosen this path. "Thank you, Your Grace."

Forgetting the need for tears, or a demure manner, she placed her hand on his sleeve and walked beside him into the dinner room. Her hand warmed, his body heat seeping through the sleeve. Her pulse tripped as she thought of what it would be like to glide her hand up the bare skin of his arm, feeling his warmth without barriers. Out of the corner of her eye she noticed he had pulled his wits back together, his society face firmly in place. It was a travesty that she had to act like a ninny and cry, but there was no other way. She glanced at him again, her gaze following the strong line of his jaw. He would have been a wonderful choice, if only he'd accepted to honor the boon.

As he held out the chair for her to be seated, she thought, not for the last time that evening, it was an utter shame the man had no interest in ruining her.

Cʒꙶꙶ

Dinner was an excruciating affair. Course after course had been served. Rich dishes he should have enjoyed but did not. The orchestrated meal was not about the food, it was about who could outdo whom. Douglas never cared much for all the frivolity that went with society. But, in the past few years, he had grown accustomed to the games. As he listened to Lord Oglithorpe bore everyone with stories of his hounds, Douglas took a drink of dry red wine and contemplated his dinner companion.

Cicely had been on her best behavior since she had propositioned him. Of course, that didn't mean he had been. It was as if he were finally awakened from a long sleep. For some reason, ever since that moment on the dance floor, he had begun noticing small things about her. Just ordinary things, but nonetheless, they were wreaking havoc with his ability to think straight.

She smiled innocently at something Oglithorpe said, then pulled her full lower lip between her teeth. The simple gesture caused Douglas to lick his own lips as thoughts of just how her mouth would taste flickered in his mind. He should be shocked at his reaction, and he was, sort of, but he couldn't seem to stop thinking about it. Just like he couldn't stop thinking about how she had felt in his arms when they waltzed. Or how she would feel in his embrace, in his bed.

He swallowed as another blast of arousal rushed over his flesh and through his blood at the memory. The sound of her soft voice, the clean, womanly scent of her. Both were still affecting him now. He couldn't believe he'd gone this long thinking of Cicely as a little sister. Especially since not one single thought of her in the past hour had been close to brotherly. He'd been blind, but not anymore.

Other than their conversation, nothing had changed, while at the same time everything had. Douglas was sure over the last two years they had danced at least a dozen times, yet until she uttered her proposition, he never once considered her as more than a pleasant companion. Now, even watching her watch everyone else was a fascinating task for him. He'd never noticed how she did not actually participate but rather held herself back, observing, as if she wasn't part of the group. Did she feel that way? As if she were just an outsider, someone not really accepted, but not a total outcast. Not once had he suspected they had so much in common.

"Your Grace?" Lady Tremount asked.

He turned to find her studying him with jaded interest. He still regretted the affair he'd had with her the year before. When he'd realized she was sitting next to him this evening, he'd almost bolted. Felicia hadn't taken their breakup very well.

"Lady Tremount."

"I asked you if you will be attending the Enderlins' house party next week."

He stifled a sigh. For the moment at least, Felicia seemed to have forgotten her verbal attack on him. Even though she'd been married for the last decade to Tremount, she'd had numerous affairs, as had her husband. Douglas was only one of the many. When he'd broken off their brief affair, she'd told anyone who would listen what a coldhearted bastard he was. He could have saved her the time. Most people already thought of him that way.

"Excuse me, Lady Tremount. I was lost in my thoughts."

Her green gaze drifted past him to Cicely, then focused back on his face. Her eyes narrowed menacingly. "That much is evident, Your Grace."

He didn't so much as flinch, but his mind was already working hard on deflecting Felicia's interest. The woman was a barracuda and if she thought his interest lay with Cicely, she'd destroy her without a thought. He couldn't have that happen to an innocent, especially one he admired like Cicely. Worry gnawed at his gut.

"I thought of missing it because I wasn't sure if there would be anyone interesting going." He leaned closer, knowing the flirtatious smile and the lowering of his voice to intimate tones would excite Felicia. She loved the game. "Of course, if you are going, I might have a reason to change my mind. My duties have kept me busy. A diversion might be welcome."

As expected, her eyes flared with sexual interest. He hoped the disgust he felt for his former paramour didn't show on his face.

"Diversions can be fun," Felicia said.

Smiling, he settled back in his chair, smug with his victory. That is, until he noticed Cicely. She stared at him, her eyes shimmering with a combination of sadness, disappointment and pain. Before he could explain his reasoning, Bridgerton stepped up behind her.

"Lady Cicely."

She turned to greet Bridgerton and the smile she bestowed upon the earl made Douglas clench his teeth.

"Lord Bridgerton."

"I wondered if I could have a moment of your time."

Relief shone in her face. "Oh." Immediately she rose from her seat and nodded at her companions. "If you will excuse me."

Everyone bid her goodbye and she left him without a backward glance. Her back was straight, her stride graceful and reserved.

Felicia leaned closer, her flowery perfume turning his stomach. "I never thought Bridgerton would be sniffing around Lady Cicely, but then, who knows what men will do when they feel they must marry. Perhaps the mart has shrunken over the years."

"I doubt Bridgerton is spending time with Lady Cicely for that reason. They are sponsoring my cousin's newest edition to the Ware family line tomorrow." But even as he said the words, he narrowed his eyes, watching Bridgerton guide Cicely through the crowd and in the direction of the doors. At least he hoped that was the reason. But the worry of that list and her proposition, along with the knowledge that Bridgerton did need to marry, had Douglas worrying.

"Whatever you say, Your Grace. Men know things women do not. However, I can tell you the on dit about town and from the tearoom is that his mother has been pushing for a marriage, and soon. Of course, he could marry better. Perhaps they have other things in mind." She laughed gaily.

He turned to Felicia. She pulled back, the expression on her face dropping from pleasure to concern, perhaps even fear. He knew she saw in his expression to watch her tongue.

"I would hope that you wouldn't allow your speculation to hurt the reputation of a woman I think of as part of my family."

Felicia swallowed, anger and worry etching lines on her aging, painted face. How had he not noticed just how many lines were there before, or the fact she was a nasty, hateful woman who wore contempt like a cloak. "Of course, Your Grace."

He joined the conversation after that, even as his mind drifted back to Cicely. What did Bridgerton have to talk to her about?

CR8O

Cicely drew in a deep breath of the fresh night air and allowed her nerves to relax. The aroma of new blooms washed away the sickly sweet perfumes and powders of the women inside. She sighed. Sighing was a great means of relaxation. The louder it was, the better she felt. On so few occasions could she get away with the action. Here she was alone and could enjoy a moment of respite.

She stared off in the distance, watching a small fountain spew crystal-clear water from a spout. Fate had never been kind to her, saddling her with an insane mother, an inattentive and gambling father and her plain features. Intelligence, humor and an inquisitive mind, she had those as well. She supposed those almost made up for her hurt.

Almost.

But, tonight, reality had been especially cruel. Less than an hour after refusing her request, Douglas sat at dinner making an assignation with a woman who had the morals of an alley cat. The claws of one as well. Rejection was hard enough, but to be slapped like that...

She wondered now how many times that had happened. How many times had men used her as a shield from other women intent on marrying them and then as a cover so they could make their own plans for the seduction of another woman? She shuddered as she pushed the idea aside, not wanting to contemplate the number.

"You didn't look as though you were having a good time."

She jumped a bit at the sound of Bridgerton's voice. Irritation swept through her, even though she felt guilty for it. She had been enjoying her privacy. She spent so much time alone, one would think she should savor every moment of social contact. But right now she didn't feel like it. She swallowed her pride. He had, after all, saved her from breaking down in tears.

She didn't need another humiliation tonight. Taking in one more breath of air, she faced him.

He leaned against the wall, his arms crossed over his magnificent chest, his expression serious. She smiled. He'd always been decent to her.

"No, I wasn't. The season is sometimes tiring."

He dipped his head once, in agreement. "I agree. I tend to think only intelligent people notice that."

"Thank you for the compliment, Lord Bridgerton."

He smiled at her formality and she could not help but return the gesture. "There is a part of me that thinks that maybe this will be my last season."

His brow drew down in a frown. "Now, don't let Ethingham's antics drive you from your friends."

She laughed, although there was no humor in it. "The friends I have do not go about in society. They keep to themselves, except for attending The Historical Society. No, I think this will be my last real season. It is wasted time, money and energies."

Bridgerton tried to call to her humor with a smile and a wink. "You can't just yet. You know with your dowry and intelligence, you should be the catch of the season."

She shook her head, but said nothing.

"Besides, Sebastian wouldn't be happy to think he was to be saddled with Anna. She drives him, and just about everyone else, mad."

She laughed. "Anna might hurt you if she heard your comments."

His facial features relaxed and he joined in. "Agreed." He paused, then stepped forward offering his arm. "I believe the orchestra is about to start another waltz. Would you do me the honor of this dance?"

She studied him, regarding him without the blinders of friendship. For the first time in several years, she realized just how handsome he was. Almost as tall as Douglas, with light brown hair, golden brown eyes and a ready smile, he'd captured the eye of many debutantes. He was known for his taste in clothes, his love of horses and his way with women. But not once had she heard anything about his kindness. She smiled, this time with true feeling.

"Thank you, Daniel. I would love to."

Their gazes caught, understanding in his for her situation. Deep down in her soul, she knew he had detected her feelings for the duke, but he had been too much of a gentleman to mention it directly. She should feel embarrassed, but instead, she felt only appreciation for the kindness he offered and for his respect.

As he escorted her to the floor, she tried her best not to look for Douglas. She had to move on. Douglas was off the list but there were many more where he came from. She needed something to acquire their attention, and she knew just the woman to help her.

CR80

After several more hours, and an overly long carriage ride home thanks to the thick fog, Cicely approached Anna in her room. She knew it was late, but if she didn't do it now, Cicely was sure she would lose her nerve. After knocking, she entered on Anna's command.

"Cicely. Come in. Did you have a good time tonight?"

"Yes, I did. Thank you." She shut the door behind her and followed Anna to her bed. When both of them were sitting on the edge side by side, Cicely gathered her courage. "I have a favor to ask of you."

Anna's blue eyes widened and filled with anticipation. Her breathing kicked up a notch. Cicely bit back a chuckle. There was nothing Anna liked better than a challenge.

"I have decided that I need a new look."

"Truly?"

Cicely nodded.

Anna jumped off the bed and clapped. "Oh, this is going to be so much fun. I have wanted to drag you to the modiste but Mother said not to bother you with such things. And when I asked Sebastian he said that I would drive you batty inside of five minutes. When I asked him what he meant by that..." She stopped talking and bit her lip, pink coloring her cheeks. "I guess I can see his meaning."

Not wanting the younger woman to feel badly, Cicely tried to soothe her embarrassment. "No. No, Sebastian has gotten a little...staid since taking over the role of earl."

Anna giggled. "Yes he has. Could you have imagined a man like him would be lecturing me on being too flirtatious? Like he has room to talk."

"It is much different when it comes to how your sister acts."

Anna wrinkled her nose. "It's a double standard if you ask me." She smiled and rushed forward. "We will go tomorrow, right away for your new clothes. This will be so much fun! Thank you for trusting me. Tomorrow. It will take forever to get them ready with the season in full swing. We must not dawdle."

"The baptism is tomorrow, Anna. We cannot go."

She frowned and tapped her bare foot. "Oh, pooh. But that is only a small portion of the day. We could go afterward, couldn't we?"

Cicely chuckled despite her worries. When Anna had first moved into the Penwyth townhouse, Cicely had felt a bit overwhelmed and somehow lacking when in her presence. When Cicely realized that it was her own feelings of inadequacies, not anything Anna had done, she had tried her best to ignore her own feelings and not to project them onto Anna. Over the past two years, she'd come to understand that Anna was actually quite smart, but many people missed it because of her bubbly personality. They missed the depth of her feelings, being bombarded with her energy.

"I think it would be in bad form to leave the baptism of your niece, Anna." She couldn't hide the humor in her voice.

"Okay, but I expect to go the day after tomorrow. We are definitely going to cut some of that hair."

Her hand went to the knot of hair at the back of her head. "Cut my hair?"

Anna smiled. "Don't worry. You have to trust me on this."

"I do, but my hair?"

"I guess we should get to bed."

Cicely blinked, a little taken back by Anna's change in direction. "Yes, it is late and we have an early morning."

Before she knew what Anna was about, she'd grabbed Cicely by the hand, pulled her off her bed and walked her to the door. She picked up her candle, handed it to her and then continued. "I will take care of everything, get all the appointments set up, arrange our coach. All of it!"

Alarm was setting in. All she had wanted was help with choosing gowns. "Anna—"

But Anna was already opening her door and practically pushing Cicely into the hall. "All will be well, Cicely. Don't worry. We'll have great fun. Rest well."

Before she could respond, Anna shut the heavy walnut door in her face. Cicely blinked, trying to grasp what just happened. She'd believed she needed Anna's help, but as she walked into her own room, Cicely thought she might have just made a huge mistake.

Chapter Three

In which our hero must pay the piper.

Douglas alighted from his carriage and frowned at the bright sun shining down. An unwelcome change, that. His empty stomach roiled as he closed his eyes and took deep breaths. Maybe drinking himself into a drunken stupor the night before had not been the best idea. He'd thought it brilliant at the time. Now, the sun was vivid while his mood was sour.

When he seemed to have gotten his body under control, he opened his eyes and tried to ignore the needles of pain shooting through his head. He swallowed and walked slowly up the stairs to the Penwyth townhouse. Fitzgerald, their pleasantly aged butler, answered the door.

First-rate was how Douglas would describe Fitzgerald. A true gem.

Fitzgerald noticed everything and commented on nothing. "Your Grace."

"Good morning, Fitzgerald." As Douglas stepped over the threshold, the scent of lemons from a fresh waxing assaulted his senses. He pressed his lips together and reminded himself that vomiting in the foyer was in bad form.

Fitzgerald took one brief look at him and ushered him into Sebastian's library. He drew a gauzy drapery over both windows, blocking out some of the painful sunlight. "I will get Cook to whip something up for you, Your Grace."

"You are a treasure, Fitzgerald." He sank into one of the chairs facing the hearth, away from the towering windows. "I don't suppose you will change your mind and come work for me?"

"I am sorry, Your Grace." He chuckled. "Lady Penwyth said that if I left she would never be able to cope." Dishes clattered in the distance. "I fear she may be right."

A moment later, he heard Fitzgerald's retreating steps. Sinking further in the chair, savoring the creature comfort, the creaking as the chair adjusted to his weight, Douglas closed his eyes, crossed his arms over his chest and tried to ignore the pain.

Why did he have to pick last night, of all nights, to drink too much? He'd actually arrived home early, slinking out of the ball, avoiding Cicely and Felicia. His relationship with Felicia had not been the high point of his life, but he had never felt as disreputable as he had when he realized just how Cicely saw him. For some reason, her disappointment made him feel worse about his behavior.

Last night, as he lay in his large bed, he couldn't stop thinking about her. The feel of her against him, the way her face lit up when she smiled, the way it had fallen... He couldn't fathom why his regard of her had changed, but he'd begun thinking about things he had no right thinking about her. Like, what did she look like with her hair down and just when had she started thinking of him as a candidate to take her virginity? Why had she decided to give that gift away? Why did she have a list of prospects?

What did she sound like when she moaned in pleasure?

He groaned when he realized he was half aroused. Again. Shifting in his seat, trying to ease the tightness in his trousers, he decided it had just been too long since he had bedded a woman.

Disgruntled with the whole situation, he rested his chin on his chest and tried to go to sleep. But, as his mind drifted and he felt his body relax, a feminine voice drifted to him.

"Darling, just what have you got there?"

The female voice was low, throaty, and it shivered down his spine. There was something vaguely familiar about it, but he couldn't figure where he had heard it before. He didn't know who she was talking to; he heard no male voice answer. His body, already aroused, shimmered with heat as the woman continued talking.

"You are such a naughty boy, you know that?" She laughed. There was a hint of coyness in it that most courtesans would have killed to be able to imitate. "You shouldn't pull on my dress like that. You might ruin the seamstress' hard toils."

Again, her laughter reached him. Ignoring the pain pounding through his brain, Douglas got to his feet and moved stealthily toward the door. He couldn't fathom what pulled at him, why he had to know who she was, but for some reason he did.

"You know, one of these days you will get in trouble for that, my lord. Naughty boy."

Her tone teased his brain. Perhaps he had met the woman sometime before. A house party or maybe a dinner that Colleen and Sebastian had held. The Wares were not that big on entertaining but they did have a few parties, and Colleen always made it a point to invite him.

"Now, if you will be a very good boy, I will give you a treat."

Her voice deepened and coaxed him closer. Normally, he would have been completely embarrassed by his actions, and he was certain he would be at some point, but he was too enticed by just who this woman was to care about the ramifications of his actions. Douglas inched closer to the door, trying not to make any noise. He stepped to the opened doorway and drew up short as he came face-to-face with Cicely.

She took a step back. "Your Grace. I hope you will excuse that I do not curtsy since I have my hands full at the moment."

It was then that he noticed Charles, Viscount Penwyth, Sebastian's heir, in Cicely's arms. And just for a second, one little split second, he wanted to believe she wasn't the one he'd heard, that he was mistaken. He wanted the woman with the teasing laugh to be someone accessible, not someone he would never dally with. But he knew she was the one. To top it off, he felt like a reprobate because he was still half aroused from her chatter to a young boy. Charles pulled on her neckline and she winced.

"Of course, Lady Cicely."

He didn't move. He stood there staring at her. How could he have not noticed just how luminous her skin was? Ivory, with a spattering of freckles across that adorable upturned nose. Her cheeks turned a light rosy color. Her blush was probably the result of her proposal last night. Immediately, his own body reacted to the reminder, and he shifted his feet, needing to create more space between the two of them.

"Your Grace?"

He frowned. "What?"

It was then he noticed the way the sunlight brought out the golden strands interwoven throughout her hair. When he met her gaze, he was struck by the way her eyes sparkled with humor.

"You're standing in my way."

For a moment the words didn't register. When they did, his face burned with embarrassment. Without a word, he stepped back and allowed her to pass. Yet, he didn't step far enough away, because when she walked by, the clean herbal scent of her surrounded him. The lavender had not been from the gardens last night. It was her. Another spark of warmth coursed through his blood, causing him more than a little pain. His hands dropped to cover his state. This insane fixation was the last thing he needed. Grinding his teeth, he tried to think of an escape, but truthfully, there was no way he could extract himself without being an ass.

He turned to follow her into the room and was surprised to find Cicely seated on the floor, Charles in her lap. For all intents and purposes she seemed to have dismissed Douglas. Without another word, he again settled in one of the chairs positioned in front of the hearth and watched as she interacted with the toddler.

For the past couple of years, he'd always thought Cicely as reserved. No, he amended, not reserved. Unhappy. Considering what her home life had been like before she had resided with Colleen and Sebastian, her despondency wasn't so amazing. Cicely was shy with new acquaintances. She had a quick wit, but was a little too smart for the young bloods of the ton. It might have been the reason she never really "took" during the last few seasons. Of course, her immediate family didn't make it any better. Even with them gone, their presence still hung over her. An overbearing, murderous mother and a father who spent more time in gaming hells than at home, her childhood had to have been lonely. Douglas was well acquainted with that feeling.

Charles grabbed her nose and squeezed, hard. He could tell it hurt because she winced, but instead of disciplining the young boy, she laughed. Douglas smiled as the sound filled the

41

room. He liked her laugh. He liked her. He found himself relaxed and comfortable, as he had not been in a long period of time, the pain all but forgotten. Cicely continued talking gibberish to the boy. He watched, listened, mesmerized by her voice. Resting his head on the back of the chair, he closed his eyes and allowed her soft, low voice to lull him into sleep.

The last thought he had before completely drifting off was that she had the type of voice a man would like to hear in bed.

A rather loud snuffle told Cicely that Douglas had fallen asleep. She looked up at him and stifled a sigh. The man didn't have a decent bone in his body. He had been appalled by her suggestion, and that was understandable. She had thought about his reaction all night and more this morning as she'd dressed. Sitting in front of her mirror examining her features, she'd found herself seriously lacking. Douglas could have his pick of any woman in London...in England. But somehow, the fact that he had taken Lady Tremount up on her offer last night hurt worse than she thought it would. She hadn't been sure he had gone back to his former paramour until his appearance alerted her to his activities the night before.

He was impeccably dressed as always. But the dark circles under his eyes told another story, as did the pained expression that quickly crossed his handsome face when he first saw her. He'd made it abundantly clear that he had no interest in her, and she needed to remind herself of that. She counted herself lucky that she knew this now. A night she might have cherished forever would be much harder to deal with when he married.

Fitzgerald appeared in the doorway, holding a tray with a glass with what could only be Cook's concoction for hangovers. As he navigated into the room, he stopped, and the stunned expression on his face caused Cicely to smile. In all the years she had known Fitzgerald, she had never seen him nonplussed, even considering there was a good chance he had come across more than one nobleman sleeping off a night of drinking.

"Fitzgerald." She kept her voice low as not to disturb Douglas, even though there was a part of her that wanted to shout just to startle him. He really did deserve it.

The butler jumped at the sound of her voice. He hadn't noticed her. It was something that happened all the time. She sighed as she gathered Charles up and stood. She smiled reassuringly as she approached Fitzgerald.

"His Grace fell asleep. Why don't you just leave that on the table beside him? He'll wake sooner or later and need it." She nodded in the direction of the side table. Fitzgerald, his eyes a bit dazed, his face ruddy from embarrassment, agreed. He set the glass on the table and walked out of the room.

Charles fussed a bit, signaling that he might be in need of a nappy change. Taking one last look at Douglas, she smiled. In sleep, he appeared younger than his years. Or perhaps, she thought standing there studying him, he actually looked his age. That made her a little sad for him. Douglas may act the rake, but there was something else there, something that made him years older. It wasn't his station exactly. It was a burden he wore without choice.

He shifted in the chair, trying to get comfortable, moving this way and that. When he settled, a smile of satisfaction curved his lips. Her heart tripped a beat at the sight. She resisted the urge to wander closer and brush the lock of hair from his forehead. Biting her lip, she turned away from temptation. Even if he did want her, she would be hurt in the end. A liaison with Douglas would not be a smart thing.

Pity, but Cicely was after all a very practical woman. Falling in love with a man like Douglas could be her breaking point.

Considering her life the last few years, that told her a lot about the situation. Her wits were all she had left. And those same wits told her that Douglas was not for her.

CR80

The one they called Raven sat by the window in his library. Sunlight brought out his sunken cheeks, his pasty complexion. His hair, once full and as dark as the bird for which he was named, was now thinned and white. It was a shock to the group assembled around him to see just how sick he was.

"Quit standing there hovering. I'm not dead...yet." His raspy voice flowed over the gathering, startling them out of their daze.

Jupiter knew each one of them feared why they may have been called. It was a significant risk, this meeting. The gravity of that alone weighed heavily on all in attendance. As he sat in a chair facing the two young heirs of their former members, he decided to be blunt.

"There seems to have been a breach."

Raven shifted, then coughed into an embroidered kerchief. "What kind of breach?"

"It seems that someone was keeping a diary of our activities during the Terror."

The room descended into silence as each man contemplated the implications of what had just been said.

Noir's heir spoke up first. "Who?"

"He was known at the time as Scarlet, but you would have known him as Baron Chambers. He died, with no heirs, as did the barony of the estate."

Silence again, but it was quickly broken by Apollo's heir. "I understand why you two," he said, nodding to Jupiter and Raven, "would be worried. But what does this have to do with us?"

Noir's heir shook his head in disgust. Apparently he knew the implications, knew what it could mean to them. He just might be useful.

Jupiter shifted his attention back to Apollo's heir. "Because, my dear boy, if word ever got out that your father was a traitor, your whole life would be ruined. You might be stripped of your title, certainly your wealth. And since you seem to have an affinity for both actresses and gaming hells, I would think you would want to hold on to both."

As expected, the young man paled as the full comprehension of his predicament materialized in his slow mind. Slow just as his father was, Jupiter thought.

"Why are you worried about it? Does it name our fathers' names specifically? Does it name anyone specifically?" Noir's heir asked.

Restless, Jupiter stood and walked around the room. "No, the names are not mentioned, but to date, I have no idea how many clues to our identity could be in there. A smart person might be able to decipher who we are. I found out about it through a rumor at The Historical Society."

"The Historical Society?" Raven queried.

Jupiter ignored him. If the man had been the leader they had needed at the time, their plan would have succeeded and worry about being discovered, moot. The fact Raven was dying a slow, painful death was the only balm to Jupiter's outrage. Instead, he stopped his pacing and turned his gaze to the two young men he planned to use.

"Yes. There seems to be a buzz about a Lady Cicely Ware. She found a diary of a traitor, who plotted with others to overthrow the King of England."

"And what do you need from us?" asked Noir's heir.

Jupiter smiled as he witnessed the same cold calculation in the young man's eyes that Jupiter felt in his bones. This one could be useful. He could be groomed.

"I want you to get that diary by any means possible. I don't care how, or who gets hurt. We must destroy it before it destroys us."

Chapter Four

In which Lady Cicely's secret is discovered.

Two days later, Cicely found herself regretting her impulsive request asking Anna for help in a self-inflicted makeover. She studied the exuberant younger woman as they traveled by coach to Madame Genevieve's shop. They bounced and jounced in the carriage, all the while Anna did not stop talking even for breath. She chattered on and on about everything. While she spoke, Cicely thought of their childhood and the few times they had been in each other's company. They had always gotten along, although there were times that Anna overwhelmed Cicely's quiet existence.

Anna had always intimidated Cicely. Her beauty, kindness and her ability to talk to almost anyone was a constant reminder to Cicely on just how badly she was lacking. Not that she would ever tell her cousin. Anna would be horrified if she knew how her older cousin felt. Besides that, Anna should never feel ashamed of her boisterous personality. Some people were simply more outgoing than others.

Everyone had different talents. Fashion was not one of Cicely's strong suits. She knew she required help. She understood little of what was in style, cared even less about it. But, truth be known, she needed something more than her sparkling personality to entice a man. Though she did not agree with the idea, clothing or lack thereof did indeed seem to attract men or at least caught their roving gaze. And that was what she needed. A few good gowns would help. Hers were serviceable. She needed stunning. Perhaps a daring neckline or two to showcase her assets. Let men know what she had to offer. Deflowering her was probably not at the top of every bounder's list. Douglas had proven that the other night. For her plan to succeed, a change in appearance was called for. Her six and twenty years had taught her if something did not work, one changed one's approach.

"I hope this means you have decided to take the dowry Sebastian settled on you seriously."

Her aunt's patient voice broke through her musings and Anna's chatter. Cicely focused on Victoria, thinking, not for the first time, that she'd been lucky in relations—if one ignored her deceased parents. From the moment Sebastian had become earl, Victoria had made certain Cicely was included in everything, even after her mother's actions had been revealed. For that, Cicely would be forever grateful.

When she didn't say anything in response, Victoria offered her a secret smile—one Sebastian claimed was a sure sign his mother was planning something. Something dangerous.

"Cicely, you know that you don't have to be frugal when it comes to your needs. Sebastian would never hesitate to pay your bills."

Embarrassment sent a rush of heat to her face. She knew a soft pink stained her cheeks. Perhaps daring necklines were not the wisest choice. Oh, how she hated being the poor relation. It seemed that for most of her life she'd been standing on the outside looking in, even when she was accepted.

"Of course Sebastian would. It isn't that at all." She could no longer stand the pity in Victoria's eyes, so Cicely stared out the carriage window. "It is that most of this is of little to no use to me and I hate to waste the money. One season and then discarded. I've always thought it rather silly and frivolous."

"But now you have had a change of heart," Anna said, her voice bubbling over in excitement. "Once Mother and I are done with you, you will be an Original."

Feeling once more in control of her mortification, Cicely turned her gaze to her cousin and tried not to frown. Anna had voiced this misconception several times since she agreed to help. There was no way for Cicely to dispel her of the notion. Her reasons for asking for a wardrobe now would shock her cousin and alarm her aunt. Cicely had no doubt at all that both of them would go to Sebastian about it. She hated lying to them, but it was the only way.

Forcing a smile and a lighter tone, Cicely said, "Really, Anna, I think I will hardly be that but I appreciate both of you trying."

As the carriage slowed, Anna offered her a blinding smile. "We shall see."

The door opened and the liveried footman offered his hand, helping all three ladies down. People brushed past them on the busy city street. A familiar throb of panic beat at the pit of her stomach, fluttering about like a trapped butterfly. She followed closely behind Anna and Victoria. Cicely hated situations like this, hated fittings. She was proportionately hard to fit, and her mother had made sure she understood what an embarrassment it was.

As she stepped into the shop, from walkway to tightly threaded carpet, her heart tripped and she felt the blood drain from her head. It was ridiculous really, but the humiliation she'd suffered years earlier always reared its ugly head whenever she was faced with shopping for dresses.

"Ahh, Lady Victoria, Lady Anna. I am so pleased to have you here today." A slender woman somewhere in her mid-thirties rushed forward, her arms outstretched. To grab or to herd, Cicely was uncertain. "I received some wonderful new fabrics for you to consider. I think they will be stunning."

Stunning? Cicely almost brightened.

Victoria smiled. "That's wonderful, Madame Genevieve. But our main goal today is to have my niece, Lady Cicely, fitted for a new wardrobe."

Madame Genevieve turned her attention to Cicely, her sculpted eyebrows rising slightly. Heat infused Cicely's face but she refused to look away. She knew she was no beauty. It was something she had faced early in life—thanks to a brutally tactless mother.

There was just a beat of silence before the dress-shop owner's lips curved into a dazzling smile. "We have just the thing."

"I thought that something in a darker shade would be better," Anna offered. "It would bring out her colors. The dark of her eyes. The light of her hair."

Cicely glanced at her younger cousin. "I've always worn pastels. They are in fashion, especially this year."

"You will wear what I tell you to wear." This came from Madame Genevieve. She had stepped closer to Cicely, her narrowed gaze traveling down her body, pausing at her chest then continuing on the path. "Pale colors make you appear sallow. Your cousin is correct in suggesting a darker wardrobe."

Without another word, the dressmaker turned and walked to the back of the store. Out of the corner of Cicely's eye, she noticed her aunt and cousin had taken a sudden interest in a particularly ugly piece of fabric.

"Come!"

Madame Genevieve's voice caused Cicely to jump. When Cicely found the woman staring impatiently at her, she hurried to do her bidding. She followed her back into the dressing area and waited until Madame shut the door.

"You will take off that offending piece of clothing." Madame's nostrils flared as if insulted by Cicely's drab garments. Cicely hesitated. It had been years since she had undressed for anyone but her own modiste and her lady's maid, Betsy. "You will let me disrobe you, Lady Cicely. I assure you, you have nothing I have not seen before. *Suivez-moi. Tout de suite.* We have much to do."

With that, she placed her hands on Cicely's shoulders and turned her in a full circle. Within just moments, Cicely stood in nothing but her shift. Again, the other woman studied her. She cocked her head to the side.

"Why do you bind your breasts?"

The question took Cicely by surprise, though it shouldn't have. It wasn't like she didn't know that every morning she wrapped the linen around her bosom. But no one, not even Betsy, said a word of it to her. It was just...understood. Asked so bluntly though, Cicely had to work her brain around the question to answer it.

"My mother said I should, as did my modiste."

"This is wrong. *C'est dommage de cacher telle beauté.*"

Cicely frowned at that. She didn't understand all the woman said but it was something about hiding things. A blush crept up her neck and warmed her face. While this modiste was at least pleasant, it only reinforced Cicely's negative self-impressions. She'd never been comfortable with her form and

51

discussing it with a woman she did not know wasn't something she wanted to do. Noting the militant expression on the other woman's face, Cicely realized that she would not let it go.

"My mother explained that I was disproportioned. I have done my best to cover the flaws."

Genevieve settled her hands on her hips and raised one eyebrow. "What you do here, this is not healthy. Things must breathe. Beauty must show."

"I will not be mocked because of my figure. The ton has enough ammunition, I will not give them more. The fashion is not favorable to women with larger...attributes."

With a string of muttered French phrases—which had to be naughty, but languages had never been Cicely's forte—Madame Genevieve turned on her heel and sashayed out of the room. "Who, I ask you, is the modiste? Eh? Who knows fashion?"

A moment later, the door opened to reveal her aunt, who wore an expression of acute concern. Behind her stood Genevieve, her expression dark.

"You will talk to the young lady. I will never allow her to wear one of my creations while doing something unhealthy and stupid."

She left them alone but Cicely could still hear her muttering in French as she walked to the front of the store. Embarrassment drenched the silence. Victoria cleared her throat, stepped into the room and closed the door gently behind her. She examined Cicely closely, concern wrinkling her brow.

"Genevieve said that you have been binding your breasts."

Cicely said nothing. The bindings were obvious standing exposed as she was. Thank heavens her cousin had not come in.

"How long have you been doing this?"

Self-consciously, Cicely crossed her arms over the offending body part—or parts, she wasn't quite sure of the proper English—and broke eye contact. This was the most discussion she'd ever had about her bosom, save that first horrendous one with her mother.

"Since about the age of four and ten." The tone of her voice was weak, and she hated that. At least it had not broken. Still, she resented that she once again sounded like that fourteen-year-old girl who didn't understand the changes in her body. She swallowed past the hate and anger of having lived with confusion and shame, for having a mother who made her feel dirty for something she knew now was natural.

Victoria moved closer, gently taking Cicely's hands and pulling them from her body. Chancing a hesitant and hooded glance at her aunt, she recognized the look on her face as one of understanding. At least it wasn't pity because that she would not be able to handle. Understanding was hard enough.

"Tell me, why did you do this to yourself? I agree with Madame, this is not healthy."

She swallowed. Truth. "My mother said that I was an oddity."

The sigh that escaped her aunt's lips sounded resigned. "Let's sit over here and discuss this."

Cicely followed her to the settee and settled rigidly next to her aunt. "No matter what you say, I know that fashions these days are not good for a figure like mine."

Her aunt's laugh took her by surprise. "Fashion is a fickle, fleeting thing. However, darling, being shaped as I suspect you are is always in fashion, at least with men." When Cicely didn't join in, Victoria sighed again. "I do not wish to speak ill of the dead, but your mother was not well."

"Up until the last, she was normal."

"I knew your mother before she married your father. We were of the same age, but never really took to each other. But, darling, you have to understand, your mother was always a vindictive harpy. Even before."

For a moment or two, Cicely could not speak. Her aunt was known for her diplomatic nature.

Victoria took one look at Cicely's expression and chuckled. "I cannot lie about your mother, not in this case. She was always spiteful and mean-spirited. She could not accept that another woman might be prettier or smarter. The tales of her come-out year would surely curl your toes. Not with delight, but with horror. I am not saying this to upset you, and I am not lying. Your mother had reason to make you feel ashamed of your figure. She had reached what society would claim to be her peak, and her daughter was developing into a beautiful young woman.

"That alone was enough to drive your mother over the edge. Add in your father's taste for cards, always searching for the next good hand to make it through to the next quarter allowances... Your mother was not a happy woman. Competing with you would have been too much. She had to take that element out of it. Or some of it."

"I understand what you are trying to do, Aunt. I appreciate it." When Victoria seemed ready to protest, Cicely stopped her by squeezing the older woman's hand in a sign of affection. "No, I do not want false comments about my appearance. While I know you are more than likely correct about my mother, I have my own mirrors. Every morning as I dress I see in great detail just what and where I lack."

Narrowing her eyes before she stood, Victoria pulled Cicely off the settee. Victoria positioned Cicely in front of her, looked over Cicely's shoulder and caught her gaze in the mirror.

"Tell me what you see."

"A plain woman of advancing age. I see a spinster nearing the shelf."

Victoria tsked. "Do you know what I see? I see a young woman with a quick mind."

Cicely snorted. "Yes, and that is all the rage amongst men. They love a woman smarter than they are."

"Oh, Cicely, all women are smarter than men." Victoria shook her head. "But there is more, much more to you. While you have physical beauty, I know you don't want to hear about it. Still, it is what I and many others see. More than that, I see a woman with hidden beauty. You only need to know how to show it to the world."

Cicely opened her mouth to argue, but Victoria tightened her hold on Cicely's arms.

"Allow Genevieve to do her work. What can it hurt? You have nothing to lose and everything to gain."

That struck too close to the heart of the matter. Her reputation was already tattered with the rumors of her mother's behavior and her father's gambling. Douglas thought her wanton. Perhaps she was. Her season would soon be over. She would go back to her books and her quiet life when the season closed. What would it hurt? This was her chance.

"Okay."

Victoria beamed at her, released her and pulled Cicely into her arms. The tenderness of the embrace, the true and unconditional love that she had never experienced before living with Victoria, caused a lump to form in her throat. Warmth filled her soul, her heart nearly bursting with happiness. Tears burned the back of her eyes as she slid her arms around her aunt and returned the hug.

When she pulled away, Cicely noticed Victoria looked a little teary eyed herself. Tugging out a linen handkerchief, she dabbed her eyes and offered Cicely a shining smile.

"Trust me, Cicely, this will work out for the best."

Cicely smiled but said nothing. If her aunt knew her purpose in all of this, she would put a halt to it. Cicely couldn't take Victoria's disappointment if she should find out her motives. Instead, she nodded and patiently awaited Madame Genevieve's return.

CȜ𝒪

Douglas offered a small smile and inclination of his head as he slid past another matchmaking mama, thinking he'd been dashed stupid for showing up at this ball. He hated the inanity of the ton and their amusements, had from the moment he made his debut into society years earlier. Already in possession of his full title, he had learned early on what that meant in society. The ruthless social climbers wanted his title—not to mention the deep coffers the dukedom held. If his stark upbringing had not prepared him for being considered a stud that could be bought and sold like any horse at Tattersall's, his first year in society would have wiped any misconceptions away.

Shaking off his morbid thoughts, he took a glittering cut-crystal flute of champagne from a passing footman and wandered around the edges of the large dance floor. He tried his best to appear inconspicuous as he looked for the object of his hunt. She had yet to make an appearance at this evening's function but he had heard she would be in attendance. He hoped she would hurry, he had already had to fend off Lady Tremount, several mamas and two recent widows. The sooner he talked to Cicely, the better.

The thought that he'd braved one more ball just to find his quarry absent left a cold ball of irritation in his stomach. He had decided to wait only thirty minutes more when he heard her name announced. He threaded his way through the crush of people to get a better view of the entrance. The moment Douglas saw her, the tension he did not even realize had gathered in his belly released, and a flood of heat wound through his blood. Flanked by her aunt and cousin, Cicely descended the staircase.

Again, he was struck anew by how he had missed certain things about her over the years. He had mistakenly allowed her to be placed into the category of family—making her off limits.

He sighed. No, he had never seen her exactly that way, but he had never noticed her beauty before. It was quiet, not so overwhelming as Lady Tremount's looks. It also did not fit into the perfect rosebud appearance of Lady Anna. Instead, Cicely's darker coloring seemed to make her appear drab, especially in that horrid pale pink gown. But a quiet shimmer of beauty lurked beneath the surface. The right man would show her just how to blossom.

Every muscle in his body went rigid. The thought that another man, some nameless, faceless bastard, would be the one to tap into her beauty, her pureness, her love, had a red tide of anger coursing through him.

"Good evening, Your Grace."

He turned and noticed Lady Catherine Hendridge and her cousin, Lady Diana standing to his left. Smiling at Lady Catherine, he kept an eye on Lady Cicely and her relations as they made their way through the crowd.

"Lady Catherine. Lady Diana." He took first Catherine's hand, bending over it, kissing the air just above it. He gave the same treatment to Lady Diana's. "How wonderful to see both of you here this evening. How are you faring?"

Catherine's eyes laughed up at him. Slim, tall and light, the woman had been considered the catch on her first season out. Catherine and he shared a unique friendship. It was one spawned out of a love of the absurd and had continued through her widowhood. Her quick wit and unwillingness to remarry made her the perfect companion for Douglas.

Dressed in celestial blue, her favorite color, she drew much attention from the bounders and rakes of the ton. Both those of the lecherous and the longing. Her dour cousin, some twenty years her senior and one of the unhappiest creatures to grace the earth, Lady Diana, frowned at him. She, too, was dressed in the hideous pastels of the season. If she didn't already look like a frigid icicle, the light blue dress solidified the image.

"It seems we are in for another crush," Catherine said. "My dance card is already full."

"As it always is." He caught a look at Lady Cicely out of the corner of his eye. "If you ladies will excuse me, I see my cousin Colleen's family making their way through the throng of people. I must say my hellos."

After taking his leave, he made his way through the throng of revelers to Cicely with a determined frown. He knew he looked irritated, due to the fact that he was, but he didn't give a damn. He had dreamt of that teasing voice, the way she had smiled up at him, and it was driving him to distraction thinking another man would be offered the boon.

He stopped in mid-step, just to have the rather large Baron Wickam run squarely into his back. Casting the man a nasty look, to have one thrown right back at him, Douglas continued on his way.

He was not confronting her because he was worried someone would take his place. He comforted himself with that knowledge. What concerned him more was the threat to her reputation.

When he finally caught up with the three ladies, the look Cicely gave him was not at all welcoming. In fact, there was a bit of a militant glare in her eyes.

"Ladies." He bowed over Lady Victoria's then Anna's hand, waiting to approach Cicely last. Without a thought, he brushed his lips over her glove, his mind spinning from the warmth and scent of lavender. When he rose, he noticed the most delicious blush creeping into her cheeks. Keeping his gaze on her face, he asked, "Lady Victoria, I wondered if I could request a turn about the room with Lady Cicely."

When she didn't respond, he looked at the older woman to find her watching him with a knowing air. "If Cicely is agreeable."

He turned back to Cicely who nodded although he knew she wasn't particularly happy with the situation. Offering her an arm, he waited for her to place her hand on his sleeve, his heart doing a little kick when she accepted.

"Lady Cicely, I do believe that you have a bit of explaining to do."

She smiled at an acquaintance, an older earl Douglas knew was one of the regulars at The Historical Society. He waited, not so patiently, for her to finish her greetings.

"I have no notion what you are talking about," she said, keeping her voice just loud enough for him to hear.

He gritted his teeth. "I think you do and I wanted to warn you before you ruin your reputation. I have told no one of our conversation, but other men would not be so discreet."

She glanced around surreptitiously. "You have fulfilled your duty, Your Grace." Letting go of his arm, she curtsied. "If you will excuse me, I need to catch up with Lady Middleton about The Historical Society meeting this week."

He looked over her head toward the corner where many of the dowagers rested. When she rose, he met her gaze. "If you promise me to be careful and make no requests to other gentlemen tonight."

She smiled. "I assure you that I will not approach anyone this evening. I have since decided against my first plan." The utter sincerity in her eyes had him nodding.

Turning, she walked to the older women and his gaze drew down her form to her rear end. He was struck again by the ferocity of his need to discover what she hid under those ghastly dresses. He felt another pulse of arousal. He ignored it and thinking he had done his duty, decided to find Lady Catherine. Perhaps her humor could distract him from his current unsettling line of thought.

CB&O

The heat of the ballroom had Cicely's head throbbing. Her breath tangled in her throat and a cold chill slithered into her stomach. She hated the occasional fear she experienced in large crowds. Every now and then, the press of people caused the dammed clawing terror to rise. The evening's party was a huge success, the number of guests overwhelming. They bumped and touched, not from rudeness, but rather lack of room. She could not step but a foot ahead without jostling someone. She tried to contain her discomfort, but that compiled with the misery of seeing Douglas pursuing yet another woman was too much.

She'd witnessed it for years, but for some reason this time, after his refusal, it was painful to watch.

Needing a respite, she excused herself from Anna's group of admirers. As she pretended to drift toward the ladies' retiring room, she wandered down the hall a bit further. A sigh of relief escaped when she found the library free.

Closing the door behind her, she wandered around the darkened room, careful of the furniture. When she located the Chesterfield, she settled at one end, kicked off her slippers and closed her eyes. The fright that had threatened to embarrass her was fading. She would never understand the nature of it. It didn't happen in small confined places, or in dark rooms like her present sanctuary.

She took deep breaths, her body slowly relaxing and her fear melting away. Only to have it rush forward again when she heard the door click. Her eyes flew open and she turned to see who was at the door. She could only see the outline of a man against the brightness of the lighted hallway. Hoping that he could not see her, she held herself perfectly still, barely breathing. All hope was lost as she listened to his footsteps draw near. But it was his voice that caused alarm to race through her.

"I see you made it here before me, minx."

Chapter Five

In which our hero makes a most thrilling mistake.

Cicely's heart stuttered at the deep sound of Douglas' voice. Oh, no. No. No. *No.*

She closed her eyes against the sudden press of tears and fought the urge to stomp her foot—which would have been difficult since she was sitting. Besides, a barefoot stomp was never as satisfactory as a heeled one. The heeled one made a very satisfying thump. She allowed a frown to disfigure her face. It was dark, what did she care? Douglas thought she was that Lady Tremount. Or some other trollop. She would almost think the situation humorous, if she didn't find it so horribly painful. She'd done nothing so hideous in her life as to deserve this.

Cicely didn't open her eyes when she felt him sink next to her on the sofa. The cushion flexed under his weight. She waited for Douglas to realize he'd mistaken her for another woman as he slipped his hand over her cold, clenched fist.

"Awfully quiet, my lady. I've never known you to be so reserved."

She opened her eyes. She was positive any moment he would guess her identity and his horror would be too much to bear. But she would, just as she had a few nights before, face it. It was best to confront his disgust for her and use it as a weapon to remind herself what he thought of her. She turned her head, drawing back when she realized he'd moved closer. She blinked, then blinked again.

With the drapes closed, the room was near pitch black, and it was understandable he didn't know who she was. He expected someone else.

Douglas trailed his incredibly warm hand up her arm, his fingers gliding over the side of her bound breasts then farther up to cup her face. Gently, he pulled her closer. His heat surrounded her, warmed her, mesmerized her.

When she was just inches away from pressing her lips to his, he paused to say, "I've never known you to play reticent before. I have to say, I quite like it."

His breath warmed her face as he spoke. Guilt held her tongue. She should tell him and end this embarrassing façade. A moment later, he brushed his lips against hers and every thought of righting his misconception dissolved. A liquid-silver thrill shot through her, sending her heart beating out of control, her head spinning. Sighing, she leaned into him. This was a fear she could learn to love.

Apparently thinking it an invitation—because truly it had been—Douglas raised his other hand to frame her face completely and deepened the kiss. She twined her arms behind his neck and returned the kiss with all the passion in her heart. The feel of his tongue against her closed mouth caused her to gasp. Before she knew what he was about, his tongue was inside, tasting her...tempting her.

God help her, she was putty in his large, capable hands.

She moaned. He slipped his hands down her body to her waist then lifted her, placing her on his lap. Warmth seeped into every pore, her flesh heating, her body vibrating. This wasn't proper, that she knew. Still...

She felt his heart beat through his shirt and jacket. That he thought her someone else didn't matter. All that mattered was that at this one moment, the man she desired—and God help her, loved—desired her in return. Her, a nobody who barely turned the head of even the most boring of men. But this man, a gorgeous, seductive charmer, was kissing her as if his life depended on it. Somewhere in the back of her mind a bit of her better judgment prodded. With determination, she pushed the doubts away. She just wanted to be touched...to feel, to be felt.

He slid his hands to her back, urging her to him. She shifted her weight, rubbing her chest against his. Even through the fabric of her gown and the layers of her binding, the friction hardened her nipples. Her bones melted as he moved from her mouth to the delicate skin just below her jaw. His lips felt so good. They burned a trail wherever they touched and when they slid from one spot to another, the fire lingered, pushing deep past her defenses, ingraining in her memory. Wanting—needing—more, she tipped her head to one side allowing him better access to her throat. He murmured something against her skin that she couldn't grasp, but it thrilled her just the same. He moved on to her ear as she began to shift against him. The scrape of his teeth against her lobe had her moaning his name and threading her fingers through his hair.

"Catherine."

The sound of another woman's name on his lips, in a voice deepened with arousal, had the same effect as a bucket of cold water. Shame filled her as she realized that while Douglas thought her someone else, she had known the truth all along. And she had allowed him to think she was that other woman. She'd believed she could accept that. She was wrong.

Pulling away, she stumbled off his lap and landed with a thump on the floor.

"Catherine?"

Arousal still threaded his voice. She sensed him looking at her and she knew at any moment she would be discovered. Oh, lud, she didn't want to face his pity and revulsion. She bit her lip to keep silent. She scrambled to her feet, bending to grab her slippers, then rushed to the door.

"Catherine!"

She couldn't say a word because there was no doubt he would know who she was, but she did hear him rise to come after her. Panic gripped her insides as she fumbled with the doorhandle. When it gave way, she hurried through the door, praying no one was in the hallway. Thankfully, for once in her life, the angels actually heard her stricken prayers. Without a backward glance, she slipped down the hall to the retiring room and breathed a sigh of relief upon finding it empty. After donning her slippers, she took in her appearance in the glass and gasped. A flush stained her cheeks, her lips were swollen and her eyes shone.

She looked like she'd been ravished, which was partially true. She would never confess it had been her. Before she could contemplate her excuses for being absent for so long, the door opened and three debutantes came rushing through, giggling.

They came to an abrupt halt in the doorway, two of them running into each other. If her nerves weren't so frazzled, Cicely was sure she would have found it funny. Still, she offered them a smooth smile then scooted around them and out the door. It was time to return to the ballroom and pretend nothing at all had happened.

03&0

Douglas rushed to the door and into the hallway only to find it empty. He settled his hands on his hips. His shaft still throbbed from the encounter and his body burned. He'd never been so aroused from just a simple kiss.

Sighing, and trying to think of anything else to cool his ardor, he had to admit it was more than a kiss. So much more. He had never had a woman completely lose herself in a kiss. Her beautiful little moans had struck him to the core.

"Douglas."

Catherine's cool voice cut through his haze of memories causing his ardor to deflate. He turned and faced the one many called *The Angel*. She truly did have a celestial look about her with her light blonde hair, sparkling blue eyes and alabaster skin. She was usually the type of woman who attracted him. But at the moment, he couldn't understand why he felt compelled to romance a woman with such a slender figure and a confident air.

"Catherine. Where did you go?"

"I have been waiting for you."

"But—" He rubbed his forehead. "Where have you been?"

"I said I would meet you in the study."

He remembered her saying that. So who had been in the room with him? "I'm sorry, I thought you said the library."

She studied him for a moment, a look of confusion drifting over her features before resignation replaced it. "I think if you truly wanted to be there, you would have been."

No accusation laced her tone. He had been ready for a fit of jealousy, although she had never shown that sort of behavior before. Married at the age of eighteen to a man in his sixties, she was now a widow known to have lovers, but was incredibly discreet. They were the same age and had been friends since they met. It was because of that he thought he needed to give her an explanation.

"Catherine—"

She shook her head and took his hand in hers. "Do not worry, Douglas. I knew this day would come and I am relieved for it. You need some happiness in your life. You deserve it."

A burst of giggles turned their attention down the hall. Catherine gave his hand a friendly squeeze then let it go. She turned to leave.

"Catherine?"

Looking back over her shoulder one last time, she offered him a small smile. "I hope she is all you need."

With that cryptic statement, she left him. He wandered down the hall in the opposite direction and allowed his mind to drift back to the encounter in the library. Something about the woman was familiar although he was sure he had never kissed her before tonight.

Needing air, he decided to abandon the ball and go to his club. After his altercation with Lady Cicely, he was more than ready to leave. She had been his one and only reason for attending. A drink or two, perhaps a hand of cards would do him good. Within a few moments, he was in his carriage and on his way to White's. In the darkness, his mind drifted back to the feel of his unknown lady's soft, full lips pressing against his. When he licked his, he could taste her there, sweet and innocent, with a touch of seductive temptress. His body reacted immediately. Letting loose an aggravated groan, he scrubbed a hand over his face, trying to dislodge the memory. When he did, a hint of lavender mixed with a subtle undertone of woman had his senses reeling.

He knew women especially by their scent. Catherine had always favored roses, on her skin, in her bed. It hit him that he should have known who his mystery woman was the moment he had leaned closer to her. Lavender had surrounded him, but he ignored it and the implications. Until now, alone in the dark with his thoughts and his dismay.

He closed his eyes as he remembered the scent of warm lavender on Lady Cicely's skin. Good Lord, he should have known. The way she had kissed told him that she hadn't had many, if any, encounters. Innocent and enthusiastic, but completely inexperienced. He opened his eyes, then narrowed them thinking of the way she'd fled, as if the hounds of hell were after her.

She had stood in the ballroom, the picture of sincerity, and told him she had no plans to meet anyone. She'd been lying. Goddamn her to hell, she *had* been lying. Right to his face!

A rush of heated anger infused his blood. From what he had experienced, Cicely was not wasting any time going forward with her plan. She had made arrangements to meet another man. Her reactions, her moans, everything he thought had been for him was not. It had been a lie. When she discovered it was him, she had fled, thinking he would never figure out it had been her.

He smiled with no humor, thinking about confronting her at the next ball. Lady Cicely had much for which to answer to.

CRSO

Three days after the encounter with Douglas, Cicely carefully turned the page of the diary. The book itself had seen better days and she suspected whoever had been in possession of the diary had not worried about its care. She assumed they had hidden it away, not wanting anyone to know what it was. More than likely, someone had not comprehended what they owned. That might explain the sorry condition of the book when she found it for sale. It wasn't until she had read about one-third of it that the incriminating information came to light.

Cicely was more than thankful for the diary these past few days. She and Anna had found themselves without Victoria, who had come down with a cold. And with the rainy weather, all of their outings had been canceled. Stuck in the house, with little to do but read, her mind kept wandering back to her last encounter with Douglas. She knew nothing would come of it, but that one taste of passion with him had her doubting she would find someone else to replace him. If he had known it was her, even though it pained her to admit it, he would have been repulsed that he had been kissing her. But for her, she worried no man would be able to compete with him.

She sighed as she looked out at the rain-drenched streets. Water sluiced down the windowpane, the patter of it hitting the ledge a perfect accompaniment to her mood. It had been several years since she had been reduced to this level of melancholy. But the thought of finding someone other than Douglas for her deflowering just seemed to send her spiraling downward.

If only she could have kept her search cold-blooded. Men performed the task of picking a lover without giving it any more thought than choosing a new cravat. Theirs wasn't a choice of the heart, but of convenience. That was originally why she came up with a list. She knew it would be no more than one stolen moment, one interlude of pleasure—at least she hoped—with no promise of marriage or further liaisons.

She now worried that any man would pale in comparison to Douglas and that was not acceptable. This solitary chance to taste passion should not be dampened by the memory of a single kiss. One make–her-knees-weak-and-her-head-spin kind of kiss, but it was still just a kiss. Not the actual deed. Although the memory of the heat that burst between the two of them from that simple act still caused a flash of warmth to spread through her.

"Woolgathering, Cousin?"

Anna's question jolted Cicely out of her thoughts. When she looked at her younger cousin, Cicely felt her face flush with embarrassment at being caught thinking about *that*.

Anna's smile widened. "Ahhh, and it must have been something naughty to get that blush."

"'Tis nothing. I was reading over the diary again."

Anna offered the diary a nasty look. "You have had your head stuck in that book for days. It's almost as depressing as this weather."

Cicely gave her an understanding smile. Anna tended to lean toward debates on modern politics, rather than history as Cicely did. Most of the ton would be amazed to find a decidedly clever debate partner in Anna since she hid her intelligence behind a cloak of smiles and twinkling eyes—not to mention being one of the best known sources of idle gossip. "I am enjoying the intrigue of it, even if I may never know who these people are."

Anna settled in her favorite chair. She trailed her fingers over the curving scrollwork on the armrests. "Go ahead, tell me."

"You hate history."

Anna rolled her eyes. "I would do anything to break the monotony of these past few days. Even listen to history. You know you want to talk about it. So go on. Share with me."

Guilt engulfed Cicely. "I am so sorry, Anna. I know—"

Her cousin waved that away. "No. I just get a little crazy waiting around because it is raining. It has nothing to do with missing the balls." She smiled. "Of course, they do say absence makes the heart grow fonder."

"Hmm, and is there anyone in particular you are thinking of?"

Anna's smile turned radiant with a touch of devious delight. "I will tell you as soon as you tell me about that. Tit for tat." She pointed to the diary that now lay open on Cicely's lap.

"You must really be in need of amusement if you are begging entertainment from me."

Anna apparently missed her dry tone and opened her mouth to argue but Cicely laughed. "No, truly, I understand. These past few days have been a bit...tedious."

"*Cicely.*"

"There was a group of five members of the Quality who saw the events in France during their revolution and plotted to overthrow the monarchy in England."

Anna's eyes widened. "Do you think there is any truth to it?"

Cicely shook her head. "I do not know. There seems to be an interesting layer of history woven into it, some of the more significant historical highlights are mentioned with eerie accuracy..." She shrugged. "Anyone could have done that. If nothing else, it could make for an interesting work of fiction."

"Yes, it would. Imagine, five men of noble blood, conspiring against the crown during the time of turmoil." Her cousin's look turned speculative. "You know what would make a better novel?"

"What?"

"The story of how they plotted but were never found out. That would be interesting."

She chuckled. "Seriously, Anna, why would that be interesting?"

"Think. Five men, their very reputations at stake, their lives, their fortunes, and a diary that could ruin it all. That is powerful."

"Oh, it is probably just someone's active imagination, but it is fascinating. So, I have told you. Now it is your turn. Tell me about this person you would like to have grow fonder of you."

Anna sighed, one of those dreamy sighs women did when they had developed a tendre. Her expression softened. Her speech slowed. When she spoke, she seemed older, more mature. "The Earl of Dewhurst."

"Dewhurst?" Cicely had to fight the urge to laugh. Now was not the time. She tried to picture the two together in her mind. Had she ever even seen them dance? "When did you decide you were interested in him?"

Anna giggled. "Oh, it wasn't me, but him. He asked to dance with me twice, once the waltz, then a minuet. Then he asked if he might call upon me, but with the weather and Mother's illness, I decided to tell him I was not available."

"Correct me if I am wrong, but your mother is not harboring the secret of dying from the Black Death, is she?"

Anna shook her head.

Amused but not inclined to encourage the behavior, Cicely admonished her cousin, "Anna, that wasn't very nice of you."

"Mother always says a man has to learn that you are not waiting for him, that he must wait for you, before he will truly appreciate you." The bundle of energy she was, Anna jumped off her chair. The action startled Cicely. "Speaking of my mother, I need to check on her and see if she needs anything."

"Let her know I will be happy to visit with her, but I did not want to bother her."

Anna had already made it across the room. She opened the door but paused with her hand on the knob. "Cicely, do not be silly. Mother would love to have you visit. I am sure you are a welcome calm after spending time with me." With a quick wink, she headed out of the room.

Cicely closed her eyes and chuckled again. Well, Dewhurst was now officially off the list. She was not that interested in the man to begin with, but her cousin's interest sealed it. He seemed a bit boring for Anna. Again, though, maybe that is what she needed. A colorful butterfly like her cousin might desire someone calm and uninteresting to even her out. But who would stop talking first? She smiled at her imagined clash of wills.

It brought her mind back to her own situation and the smile fell from her face. If she had been plagued with errant thoughts before, after her encounter the other night with Douglas her imagination had spiraled into sensory overload. He had not called on her the last few days, so she had assumed that he did not discover her identity. Or worse, he had realized it was her and was mortified. Well, maybe not mortified, that was not a word men used when describing their feelings, but something along those lines. Horror? Embarrassment? Disapproval? Disgust?

She sighed again, trying to fight the depression that had been getting worse with the constant downpour of the last few days. Rising, she went to view it through the paned window that looked out onto the muddy street. Few people were out due to the weather. Those who were dashed about. She knew that feeling. Her own inactivity the last few days had driven her batty. She was ashamed to admit that it wasn't just the house confinement, and it was not her cousin. The truth was her knowing that each day that passed she was closer to the end of her last season and the loss of her dream of being ravished. Wherever would she find a willing man then? Her means of access would severely be shortened.

Turning away, Cicely decided to visit with Victoria, leaving her worries for another time. Sitting in a study, listening to the rain and reading an old diary would only make her depression worse. Nothing would be solved today and worrying would only frustrate her. A few more days without Douglas and she might clear her mind of the memory of the taste of him, the feel of his mouth against hers, and how thrilling it had been to lose herself in that kiss.

Even as she searched for ways to move on, to find another man for her quest, she knew Douglas would never leave her heart.

Chapter Six

In which Lady Cicely unveils a most interesting surprise.

Douglas shifted his weight from one foot to the other, waiting for Lady Cicely to arrive. Anticipation skated along his nerves and his palms were sweating. Not since he was a boy of three and ten had he had this reaction to confronting a female. At that time it was an upstairs maid named Dottie who called him sweet and pinched his cheek—and not the one on his face.

But this was different. It was more like...frustration. Being exhausted on top of that had not helped either. Since their interlude in the library, he had not seen her—at least not in the flesh. But each night he would find himself in bed thinking of her, that kiss and her reaction to it. No matter how many times he tried, he could not wipe out the memory of her sighs and moans, the way she tasted.

Douglas shifted his feet again, trying to ease the heaviness in his groin. He'd woken up more than once with a need for a woman and knowing that for some insane reason, Cicely was the only one who would be able to ease the ache. He had never been one to pine for a woman since they usually approached him. With his title, finding a bedmate was never a problem.

Now, though, he found himself waiting for a virgin who kissed like sin and was searching for a man to deflower her. Her absence from events had made it even more annoying. For some reason, she, Lady Anna and Lady Victoria had been missing from society's gatherings. He had made the rounds at every place he could think she might be but she had not given him the chance to confront her about her reprehensible behavior.

Irritation still lit through him that she had run off from him that night. He was certain she had planned on meeting someone. Trying to figure out who that someone was had driven him mad the last few nights. But she had known before she left that it had been him. He distinctly remembered her moaning his name.

With a sigh, he shifted again. At the rate he was going, he would probably embarrass himself. Trying to distance himself from that particular memory, he moved his attention to his mission to keep Cicely from enacting her stupid plan. Douglas worried that she may have already embarked upon her task of seduction with some unknown man of the ton. It was unacceptable that she ruin her fragile reputation over such an asinine plan. It must stop. He needed to know just who she had been planning to meet there, in the library, unchaperoned, in the dark. That one thought had cost him more sleep than any other.

Trying to move away from his proprietary thoughts about Lady Cicely—which seemed to vacillate between aggravation and arousal—Douglas studied the others in attendance at The Historical Society meeting. He was unimpressed. Did she really enjoy these engagements? This particular monthly meeting was being held by Lady Ballston, a meticulous leader in the bluestocking circles. Douglas repressed a shudder. Intellectual study was not his forte and while he didn't disdain the study of history, gatherings such as these caused memories of Eton to rush back into the front of his mind. Damned if he wanted to remember that hell.

"Surprised to see you in attendance, Your Grace."

He turned and found Bridgerton studying him with sharp interest.

"Why is that?"

The earl shrugged. "I had not noticed your interest in this particular study before now."

"Lately I have found myself remarkably intrigued by history." He turned his attention back to the door. It had taken plenty of coins to get one of his stable lads to frequent the kitchens of the Ware household. He was not going to miss his chance to corner Lady Cicely. He had stopped short of sending a missive to her, for he was sure it would not go unnoticed by others in the Wares' employ. Haunting her doorstep would not work either. This public venue would do nicely, however.

Today, she would not escape him. He would make bloody sure the woman explained her actions the other night. He relished their meeting.

"Hmm. I heard a delicious rumor about you."

Douglas did not look in Bridgerton's direction when he said, "Is that so?"

"Yes, I heard that you had trouble remembering the steps to the waltz at the Fredricksons' ball the other night. I remember you being distracted, but forgetting steps? That is unheard of."

The sarcastic tone caught Douglas' attention and he turned to face the other man. "I have no idea what you are talking about. Nor do any of the people saying such foolish things. Are we clear?"

"As long as you understand that your interest in history should be on an intellectual level only."

The warning in Bridgerton's voice needed no explanation. He saw the way the younger man had looked at Cicely at the ball. It had not escaped his notice that the other man had danced a waltz with her either. Knowing that it was rumored the earl's mother was pushing for a wife did not make Douglas any happier. Cicely would have to explain her behavior the other night before he would let her even consider an offer from Bridgerton.

"Do not worry, Bridgerton. I will not...intrude on your enjoyment of the genre."

When Bridgerton raised one eyebrow, Douglas realized how threatening his voice had turned. Before either of them said anything more, a rise in excited murmurs drew their attention to the entrance of the room. In droves, men and women pressed in on whatever was causing such a commotion.

"What is it?" Bridgerton asked.

"I don't know." Even at his height, Douglas could not see what the excitement was about. Both he and Bridgerton started walking to the door. When a rather large woman stepped out of the way, the sight before him made every thought of Bridgerton and a possible offer dissolve. He briefly felt lightheaded and thought that every drop of blood must have left his brain and moved south.

Standing in the arched entryway was Cicely, but not the woman he had known before. This was a beautiful, voluptuous goddess.

The first thing that drew his attention was her hair which was decidedly shorter. It barely reached her shoulders and now had a slight wave. The new style showcased her strong jaw and high cheekbones, giving her a more feminine look, less severe, softer.

As his gaze moved down her body, he swallowed, his mouth suddenly dry. The delicate layers of her day gown draped her curves, which there were—if he did say so himself—many more than he remembered. In the years he had known her, Cicely had always worn the pastels of a young debutante that had made her appear sallow. But the dark shade of pink she now wore, and the more mature style, lent an air of sensuality to her appearance he had never seen before. It brought out the golden highlights in her hair and the rosy undertone to her complexion.

"Holy Christ," Bridgerton muttered. "Where the hell did that figure come from? An utter crime to keep that under wraps."

Anger shot through Douglas and he gave Bridgerton a ferocious look. "Get your mind out of the gutter, Bridgerton."

Bridgerton rocked back on his heels, studying him, while Douglas tried to ignore the earl. "So, that's the way of it, hmmm? You truly do have an interest in, ahh, history."

Heat crept up his neck and burned the tips of his ears. He'd not blushed like this since his episode with Dottie the upstairs maid, and he would be damned if he admitted to it now. "I have no idea what you are talking about." Wonderful, now he sounded like a spurned woman. How much lower could he sink in a span of minutes?

Bridgerton chuckled. "Indeed? Then you will not mind if I call upon her?"

"I would advise against it, if I were you, Bridgerton." Anyone within listening distance would note the steel in his voice, the implied threat.

Bridgerton offered Douglas a sardonic smile. "I would say that I will not be your only competition."

With a glance, Douglas could tell that Bridgerton was correct. Men were already pressing closer. Like wolves scenting fresh blood. Not one of them had paid her a bit of attention just days ago, but now they were all acting as if she was the latest attraction at Vauxhall. A look of sheer panic passed over her face and he realized that Cicely might be close to losing control.

Even as angry as he was, he did not want her to embarrass herself. Without another word to Bridgerton, Douglas made his way in Cicely's direction. He'd save her from the slavering fools, and then they would have their chat. She'd run from him once. He was not going to let her slip from his grasp again.

Cicely curled her fingers into her hand as her throat closed and her heart rate increased. A chill sliced down her spine even as her head began to spin. She had thought she would be ready for this. Anna had told her she would cause a stir, but Cicely found the interest too much. The urge to turn in the opposite direction and run as fast as her pink-kid-slippered feet would carry her almost overwhelmed her.

She felt Anna give her a reassuring squeeze on her elbow before moving away in the direction of Dewhurst. Even though she knew her cousin was present if she needed her, she couldn't help feeling a bit abandoned. Afloat in a sea of curious onlookers. People who whispered about her when she was just beyond earshot. Those same individuals who only grudgingly accepted her into their circles now spoke with warmth in their voices.

Cicely reminded herself this was for her own good. She tried to take in air in measured pulls, not gulps. True, she wanted to learn how to work through this fear, but she didn't think she could accomplish it overnight.

"Lady Cicely." She turned and found Lord Oglithorpe talking directly to her newly exposed bosom. "I understand you recently discovered a very interesting diary."

She looked at the older gentleman who licked his dry, cracked lips and sighed. His comments confused her because she had tried talking to him a week ago about the diary and he had rebuffed her. "Yes, I have. I am still unsure of its authenticity, however."

"Lady Cicely."

Douglas' deep baritone drifted over the crowd and for a moment she did not react. She couldn't. She was frozen in alarm. She had not realized he was in the room before this, and in and of itself that was a singularly odd occurrence for her. However, it was also odd for him to attend a meeting. As far as she knew, he'd never before expressed an interest in the society.

Heat infused her entire being as the memory of their last encounter came rushing back. Crystal-clear images, sounds and tastes assaulted her senses. The memory had never been that far from her mind, but every now and then she could convince herself that it had been a dream. A rather delicious, decadent dream, but a dream nonetheless. When she turned in the direction of his voice, she found him standing closer than she expected. Their bodies brushed. Her pulse jumped and another wave of warmth threaded through her.

She curtsied. "I did not know you attended our small gatherings, Your Grace. What a pleasant surprise."

The feral smile he granted her as he bent to kiss her offered hand sent her nerves into a serious bouncing snit. "There are many things you do not know about me, Lady Cicely."

His voice had dipped, the tone slightly suggestive. A few of the gentlemen coughed to cover their chuckles and many of the women giggled. Cicely gave him a frown to let him know her feelings, though understanding she was somewhat stuck in the situation. He still held her hand, and pulling away and marching off in a huff would serve only to draw more attention to her. Lady Cicely Ware did not cause scenes, nor did she blush readily when a man flirted—mainly because none had done so before now. Since she was already doing the latter, she decided it best not to do the former.

The audience watching the byplay had not dispersed—and would not until Douglas and Cicely moved on from this ridiculous scene. As they continued to stand there, the buzzing of the crowd grew and she attempted to hurry the conversation along.

"I am surprised that in all the time we have known each other, you never mentioned an interest in history."

His smile widened and he slid his fingers over her palm to the small bit of skin visible between her glove and sleeve. As the tips of his fingers slipped into her sleeve, her breath caught. The boldness of the action spoke of his reputation as a rake. Douglas finally released her hand and a shiver of heat rushed over her flesh from the spot his fingers had caressed.

"I find myself interested in history of late."

He took her hand again and placed it on his arm. Her body still vibrated with a delicious hum. She swallowed.

Chatter started out slowly, then rose as they spread out through the room, passing from one group of attendees to another. Cicely wanted to scream. If people thought he was courting her, they would pity her when he dropped out of sight. And he would when he figured out that there was nothing he could do to deter her from her goal. He was only paying her mind to keep her from her plan. He had no interest or inclinations of any sort other than perhaps protecting her, which was sweet, but unnecessary. She had Sebastian watching over her. He was more than enough.

"Then you are indeed in luck today. Lord Oglithorpe is going to present an interesting paper on the Roman Empire."

Douglas' face paled and the muscles around his mouth tightened ever so slightly.

"Would you do me the honor of letting me escort you to your seat, Lady Cicely?"

"Of course, Your Grace."

She knew he would try and seat them in the back, away from others so he could browbeat her. That was fine by her. She was ready to let him hear a few of her complaints as well. As she stepped up beside him, he took a light grip on her elbow and led her to the third row. Surprised by this, she moved in front of him and seated herself. When he had settled in next to her, she leaned closer to him. Drawing in a deep breath, she caught a whiff of his cologne. Douglas did not douse himself in cologne, as many of the gentlemen did to hide their body odor. There was an undertone to his scent, but mostly what captured her attention was the undeniable smell of Douglas. Something so basic, so very masculine. There in the middle of the Ballstons' parlor, she wanted to bury her nose against his neck and sniff.

Again, another blush rose up over her cheeks and she had to resist the urge to cover her face in embarrassment. Really, where did these kinds of ideas keep coming from? Up until she had formulated her list of men, Cicely had never had such lascivious thoughts.

"I would really like to know what is going on in that brain of yours to cause such a blush." He spoke in a pitch only loud enough for her to hear, and even knowing that, she blushed harder.

"I have no idea what you are speaking about."

He snorted, this loud enough for others to hear. Lady Featherstone, one of the older and most conservative of Society members, twisted in her chair to give him a look of remonstration for emitting such a rude noise. Douglas made no sign that the sound had come from him, just stared at the woman. When the matron had turned to face the front of the room again, Cicely said, "Really, Your Grace, I think that this action is unnecessary. Could we not do this some other time?"

He crossed his arms over his chest, his gaze locking on hers. Hard, unbending, she knew the expression well, had witnessed it only days earlier. It was his ducal stare, the same look he had given Lady Featherstone. This time it was she who snorted. Lady Featherstone's back straightened, but she did not turn around.

"You might want to rein in your behavior," Douglas said, his voice filled with more disapproval than the look Lady Featherstone had sent him. Irritation filled her. Irritation with him, with society rules that stuck her on the shelf, and finally, irritation at herself because even knowing what an ass he was, she still wanted another kiss.

"I believe, *Your Grace*, that at my advanced age, I can decide how I would like to act in and out of public."

He said nothing, but she did not miss the flare of heat in his eyes. Even knowing it was because of anger and not desire, her body warmed, her heart doing a nice little jig. Nervously, she licked her lips again. His gaze dropped to watch the action. When he made eye contact once more, they had darkened even further.

Suddenly she could not seem to draw in a deep breath. Her clothing felt too tight, her skin as if it were ablaze. Douglas seemed to notice her condition because his own skin flushed.

She watched, fascinated at the movement in his jaw. Two muscles shifted back and forth while he ground his teeth. For a moment, everyone surrounding them melted away as she found herself mesmerized by the heat in the depths of his grey eyes. The tinge of blue around the outer edge seemed to darken the longer they stared at each other.

When he spoke his voice was hard and unbending. "Considering what happened last time we were together, I felt that being surrounded by a room full of people was a brilliant idea. Your valuable reputation and all."

Her panic mounted as she turned away. He could not know it had been her. How would a man who had probably been with scores of women be able to tell the difference between any of them? He'd even called her by another woman's name.

Without looking at him, she said, "I have—"

"Don't."

The command in his voice was unmistakable. This time when she looked at him, his expression had hardened and his eyes narrowed. And Lord help her, even that aroused her. There was something definitely wrong with her.

She smiled, although little humor showed in it. Behind her mask of complacency, her mind was jumping from one option to the other and took the only one she thought might work, even if just for the moment.

"Whatever do you mean, Your Grace?"

The muscles in his jaw moved again, once, twice…

"Just don't. You know what I mean, and if you do not take my advice, I will make sure you and everyone else in this room understands."

"Understands?" Her voice had become breathless again, as if she were a debutante who did not know how to handle herself in social situations.

"My meaning. My preference. The situation. All of it."

Seeing the very real threat in his expression, Cicely decided it best to retreat and rework her plan. When she settled back in her chair, she ignored the satisfied look on his face, because truly, she wanted to hit him. She was sure from this point on, he would be a bother. Out of some misguided sense of duty, he would hound her every attempt to find another man.

Who would have thought one rakish duke would give her such trouble?

CBEO

A man many thought they knew stood in the back of the room and watched the byplay between Lady Cicely and Ethingham with keen interest and more than a bit of humor. He had no idea what was bubbling between the two, but something was there. It surprised him that Ethingham would move in that direction. Decidedly odd for a man considered one of the best catches in London. Considering Lady Cicely, a woman with no prospects and a very bland appearance had captured his attention, it was a troubling development indeed.

Unless Ethingham had heard of the diary and had an interest in it. The young duke was not as active in politics as his predecessors had been, but he did have ties to the war department. An uncle... No, a cousin was the undersecretary of something there. Perhaps the duke was investigating and desired access to the information? A chill passed over his skin, then seeped beneath the surface, curdling the contents of his stomach. Damnit, he didn't need a bloody duke traipsing around where he didn't belong. It added another edge to the worry he had been dealing with all along.

That damned idiot Oglithorpe called everyone's attention to the front of the room, ruining his ponderings. Sighing, he thought about his next plan of action. He had tried his best to gain Lady Cicely's attention but she had ignored him, so he had developed other plans, better, less-complicated plans. He had to get ahold of that diary, by any means possible. Too much could be destroyed by its discovery. His mother, his sisters, not to mention the tenants from his estate. He didn't give a damn about the other men, but he cared deeply for his own family, especially their status in society.

The panic that had been riding his back for over a week now caused his breathing to hitch. He covered it with a slight cough. He had done a great many things to protect his family name over the years. The horrid secret he had inherited must be protected at all costs. He'd never really had regrets about his actions. Although he did feel a little guilty for misleading a woman now to save his reputation.

No, he chastised himself. He did not care what needed to be done. He would get that diary, no matter who got hurt in the process.

Chapter Seven

In which Douglas finds he must compete for attention.

"I always knew it was wrong for you to do that to yourself, miss. Not healthy. Not healthy at all." Betsy shook her head in disgust. "But your mother would have none of my suggestions, and well, after she died, I decided it wasn't really my place."

As Betsy fastened the last few buttons on the back of Cicely's dress, she continued to prattle on about the changes in Cicely's wardrobe. How she loved the design. How she herself would have chosen those darker shades. She had repeated the comment about what was her place and what was not at least ten times in as many minutes. Cicely, already nervous about her appearance at the Overton Musicale tonight, was ready to scream like a harpy and go hide in her dressing closet.

"Of course, this color is near perfect for your complexion."

That stopped her. "Really?"

"Your coloring brings out those roses, it does. Come see."

Cicely moved toward the mirror and inspected herself. Betsy was right. The ivory of her complexion set off the deep scarlet of the rose buds. They looked beautiful. She trailed her fingertips over the design. She looked beautiful. The woman in the mirror smiled. Her white teeth barely showed in a slight gap between her full lips. Her bust pushed against the fabric, and while not inappropriate by any means, Cicely still found it a bit risqué. And she liked it. She felt, for the first time in her life, like she could possibly turn a head or two when she walked into a room.

If someone had told her three days earlier that she would look so different she would have laughed. But there she stood, a gown of brilliant red hugging her newly revealed curves. The silk confection had been designed in such a way as to accentuate every single last selling point her figure offered.

She twirled in a slow circle, briefly enjoying the graceful ripples of her gown. Looking down, she reached in and tried to readjust her breasts.

Betsy slapped her hand away. "That is how the dress is designed."

She had to admit that she had never looked finer in her life. Her hand fluttered to her neck. Earlier in the afternoon, Sebastian had insisted she wear the Ware rubies tonight, more to please his wife, Colleen, than to please Cicely. He would not take no for an answer. No was a word he seemed both uncomfortable with and unable to comprehend.

She ran her hands over the beautiful, shining diamonds and rubies that sparkled against her skin. The necklace was heavy in her hand and more so on her neck, but it rested there with solid comfort. It was as if the stones represented ancestors long gone bestowing their approval on the current generation.

On her.

Everything from her styled hair, to the fancy silk slippers with the tiny rosebuds embroidered all the way around encasing her feet, made Cicely feel as if she were another woman. She caught her breath. Someone…special.

"When is the duke coming to escort you to the musicale?"

That was another thing that had her stomach doing somersaults. She placed her freshly gloved hand against her belly, mentally ordering it to settle down. Douglas had insisted on escorting Cicely, her aunt and cousin to their function tonight. Knowing he planned on lecturing her on her behavior, she had been slow in preparing for the outing, dragging her feet through the entire process.

He knew, or suspected it had been her the night in the library, their lips locked in passion in a darkened room, wantonly seated on the Chesterfield. That was mortifying enough. But the fact that he now saw it as his duty to tell her what she was doing wrong in her quest was going to quite probably drain every last bit of confidence she had gained this afternoon from her first appearance.

"My lady?"

She shook herself out of her morbid ponderings and smiled at Betsy. "He should be here any minute."

Before Betsy could hurry her along, a footman knocked on the door to announce that both her aunt and cousin were waiting with their escort.

"See?" Betsy asked.

Knowing there was no delaying her cousin, or the inevitable, she grabbed her reticule and made her way down the stairs. As she turned the corner of the staircase, she saw Douglas standing at the bottom chatting with Anna. His interest snagged by her animated cousin, he had not noticed Cicely's descent. She paused, taking the freedom his inattention offered to study him.

Dressed all in black, save his white linen shirt and cravat, he presented the picture of the perfect aristocrat. He glanced up with a mild expression of annoyance that only accentuated his attractiveness. As he started to turn back to Anna, he paused and looked back up, noticing her frozen on the stairs. For just a second—or maybe two—he did not break eye contact. The breath in her throat tangled, her heart rate tripled. Heat darkened the grey of his eyes. Then, slowly, his gaze traveled down her body. With each inch he covered, she felt naked, as if he could see through the layers of silk. By the time he met her gaze again, every nerve ending in her body quivered. Goose bumps rose on her flesh.

The muscles flexed in his cheek and a dark flush crept up into his face.

She licked her suddenly dry lips and tried to order herself to move. But she stayed transfixed, consumed by the enigmatic man who had haunted her dreams for too many years. In all the time she had yearned for it, she would have never imagined he would look at her that way. As if she were a feast and he were a starving man. She drew in a breath and his eyes almost dilated. She swore she heard a growl emanate from him. He looked ready to climb up the stairs and do something drastic.

It was at that point that Anna noticed her and clapped.

"Cicely, you look wonderful. See, Mother? I told you the scarlet would be glorious."

Anna's excited voice cut through the trance that held both Cicely and Douglas immobile. Douglas broke eye contact, turning away, giving Cicely the ability to finally finish her descent to join everyone else. Her nerves still jumped, her body still hummed, but she offered the small group a smile as if nothing untoward had happened.

"Thank you very much, Anna. I am sure everyone on Curzon Street is now well aware of your excitement."

But Cicely's droll tone did nothing to suppress the younger woman's excitement. "I told you that you would look beautiful in red, and I was correct."

"And so modest at the same time," Sebastian said from the doorway to the library.

Anna turned to face her brother. "Oh, pooh. If you had seen the way she balked at the colors Madame Genevieve and I suggested—"

"If I keep listening to you, brat, you will figure out a way to lay claim to her beauty. And looking at our cousin, I can tell you that is all natural."

Cicely smiled at her older cousin. He'd always been kind, even before ascending to the role of earl and head of the family. But in the last two years, he had become more of an older brother, no longer the distant, brooding cousin. Since his second marriage, the spark of life in his eyes was easy to see.

She curtsied. "Thank you for your compliment, Cousin."

He laughed and pushed away from the doorjamb. "Now that won't do for a Ware."

Stepping forward, he grabbed her by her upper arms and pulled her closer to kiss her cheek. These displays of familial affection still confused and bewildered Cicely, but she no longer held herself stiffly away from him. She'd had little affection from her mother and father, but since moving in with this branch of the family tree, her cousins ignored her protests and treated her as if she were a sibling.

"Sebastian, don't muss her hair," said Colleen as she descended the stairs. Tall, lithe, even after two children, and beautiful, she joined the group gathering at the bottom of the staircase, her smile as warm and welcoming as Sebastian's and Anna's.

Sebastian slid his arm around Colleen's waist and drew her nearer. Again, the Wares did not behave as much of society did. Even in front of family, signs of love such as this would never be accepted.

At the moment, as she watched the couple, she did not understand why society frowned upon it. What was so wrong with a couple who loved each other showing it to the world?

"Fine one you are to talk since you hate all the pomp of going out," Sebastian remarked.

Colleen chuckled at her husband's comment because it was well known that she would rather do anything than go to the ton's activities. When she turned her attention to Cicely, her eyes widened slightly and her smile warmed even more.

"You do look lovely, Cicely. And—even though I know I will regret it later—I have to say Anna was correct about the color. But I have to give credit to my husband for the rubies. They are the perfect touch. You wear them beautifully."

"Thank you," Cicely said.

"I see that we are all ready to go and here is Fitzgerald with our wraps," Victoria announced.

As they donned their wraps, Cicely cut a curious look at Douglas who had been unusually silent and brooding during the entire exchange. "We need to hurry to make it before they start," her aunt warned.

Within minutes, they were on their way. She sat next to Anna as Douglas sat facing her beside her aunt. Even without much light she could tell he was watching her. The look in his eyes reminded her of an animal hunting. She shivered and pulled her wrap closer to her body.

CR80

"Did you notice the way Douglas was staring at Cicely?" Colleen asked after she and Sebastian had retired to the library.

Sebastian looked up from the task of massaging her foot. Damn, but he was a lucky man. Colleen had reclined on the sofa, her hair unbound. She was his Aphrodite come to life.

"What did you say?"

She laughed. "You're so easy, Sebastian. I said, my cousin seemed to pay particular attention to yours."

"Do not think about it."

She blinked, the look of pure innocence flashing in her grey eyes. "Whatever do you mean?"

"Do not try and match them."

"Why not?"

"Douglas is way out of her league."

She gasped and sat up. "Why ever would you say something like that? She saved my life, Sebastian. If it had not been for her, I would have never survived. We would have lost everything."

Her staunch support of the younger woman warmed his heart even as the memory of that night years earlier chilled his blood.

"Now, Colleen, I just mean in experience. Your cousin does not have the best reputation. He is known to be a bit of a rake."

She sniffed at that, settled against the leather again and crossed her arms. "I know another man who was a bit of a rake before settling down."

He smiled. "Well, there is that. I am sure her appearance just took him by surprise. There is a...significant change in her figure."

"*Sebastian.* I cannot believe you said that." But he could hear the amusement in her voice.

"He is a man."

"But he had seen her earlier today at The Historical Society meeting."

That caught his attention. Briefly, he pondered it. "He attended a meeting?"

His wife nodded. That made Sebastian pause. Colleen wiggled her foot to get him to continue. As he did her bidding, he thought back to the look Ethingham had given his cousin and sighed. Ethingham was a hard man to read. He should be. He'd spent years building up the walls around him. He'd had to be three different people all the time. The proper son, regardless of his improper parents. The duke, inheriting the title too early to be easy. And the man he was with his friends. Counting himself fortunate to be among the few Ethingham considered friends, Sebastian wondered if he even knew the real Douglas.

"I don't know. I'll keep an eye on him and make sure Daniel does too."

She smiled at him. His body vibrated and his cock hardened in record time.

"Now that I have pleased you, wife, how about coming over here to please us both?"

She slid over the sofa and pressed her body against his. "I will see what I can do about that, husband." It was the last coherent thing either of them said for quite some time.

CS80

Douglas frowned at the Earl of Cummings as he once again dipped his attention to Cicely's breasts. It was the third time in less than ten minutes the fool had done that. It wasn't as if he was the only one, either. Every man who had chatted with her that evening had not been able to tear his gaze away from her chest. As if they had not seen bare flesh before.

At that moment he was ashamed of his sex. Never before had he witnessed such an embarrassing display. Granted, being a man, he understood the fascination, but he could control himself. Apparently, he was the only male in the vicinity who could. Cicely had managed to gain lustful looks from every eligible—and not-so-eligible—gentleman in attendance. From the second they'd entered the Smythe mansion, men had been buzzing around her. Their behavior was worse than the slavering idiots from The Historical Society earlier today.

As for Cicely, she had said little to those attending her, but she'd held her own. He could tell by the way she hesitated before speaking that she was nervous with the attention. Still, Douglas worried that with the interest she was garnering, she might seize the opportunity to find a willing man from her list. That he could not have, so he had stayed by her side since they had arrived. It had not deterred the men one bit.

She drew in a deep breath, attracting his notice and that of her gathered harem. The swell of her breasts rose further over the edge of her bodice and he swore he heard a sigh of appreciation from several of the men. Anger and arousal threaded through his blood. He shifted his feet to relieve the tension in his groin.

Since she had appeared on the stairs that evening, his body had throbbed. It took every bit of his willpower not to touch her. Possessiveness had driven ahead of his attraction the moment they had made their way into the crowd. It was not like him at all to act this way over a woman—especially one he had only kissed—but he could not seem to stop.

Cummings cleared his voice nervously. "Of course, I had not attended a meeting until today, but I found the discussion invigorating." His tone had turned adoring. Douglas had to fight the urge not to box the nitwit's ears.

He threw Cummings a disgusted look, but the man never noticed. A mixture of calculation and adulation colored the younger man's expression. He would probably ask to lick the bottom of her feet. Before he could point out that attending a meeting to hear another lecher talk about the Roman Empire did not make one an appropriate suitor, Lady Victoria made her way through the throng surrounding Cicely. She gave Douglas an odd look, but said nothing about his choice to guard her niece.

"Cicely, darling, your cousin has seats for us and the musicians are setting up so they should be starting soon."

"If you will excuse me, gentlemen." Cicely smiled at the hounds sniffing around her skirts then offered Douglas a look of warning. "I must do as my aunt bids."

With that, she slid seductively through the crowd, attracting the attention of every last rake in the room.

Just where had this goddess come from? She looked different, yes, but now she even moved differently. There was a sway to her hips that was not there before.

As she bent to talk to the Dowager Duchess of Fillmore, a waiter dropped a tray of refreshments, the crystal crashing to the floor. Shards of glass flew in every direction. Douglas sighed, a long one of resignation and understanding. He had a rather definite feeling accidents would become a normal occurrence from men around Cicely.

He followed her to her seat, only to find her aunt situated on one side of her and her cousin on the other. There was an open seat next to Lady Anna. Knowing that if he made an issue out of the seating people would take notice, he swallowed his objection and took the seat. After settling into his chair, he decided to do his damnedest to ignore the throb of arousal pulsing in his veins and concentrate on the music.

CŚŁĎ

By the time intermission rolled around, Douglas knew without a shadow of a doubt he was crazy. He'd lost his mind and any sense of judgment he possessed. Where he was, what he was doing proved it.

He'd sat through the singularly worst performance he had ever seen, just so he could keep a watchful eye on Cicely, worried she might ruin her reputation. Never before had he worried about virgins and their purity. The only thought he gave them was how to avoid them. But now, here he stood, watching from across the room, as a young baron fell under her spell when she smiled at him.

A tangle of lust and protectiveness, not to mention aggravation, kept him in a foul mood for most of the night. In one moment he was ready to shoot any number of the men gathering around her seeking to gain her attention. In the next, he was ready to tear that damned red dress from her beautiful, proud, pale shoulders and explore every curve barely concealed beneath.

The throb of desire that had gripped him earlier that evening would not subside. The best thing would be to leave, find a woman and relieve his torment. It had been weeks since he'd had a woman and he definitely needed the release. But the memory of that simple kiss still haunted him on a nightly basis and it was now going to worsen with the image of her in that dress. For the first time in years, Douglas had actually awakened in the middle of an orgasm. He hadn't done that since his teen years.

Cicely laughed at something Cummings said—that hound had come sniffing around her skirt again—and Douglas mashed his teeth together. Cummings was the worst sort of rake. Speculation ran high and fast through those in the know about how long it would be before the young earl ended up in debtor's prison. There were bets on the books at White's on how much longer the earl would be a free man.

With the mounting debt from his taste for cards, not to mention his expensive mistress who reportedly fancied jewels, the new earl was sinking the earldom into complete devastation. He'd lose it. The only question was how soon.

Several generations of Cummings had been known for their wanton ways. They were always fond of the drink, women and dice. But this one...this one was worse than the others Douglas had heard about. There had been rumors of a sadistic appetite that made even the most jaded Cyprian avoid Cummings.

Not that Ethingham's own grandfather or father had been much better than Cummings or his relatives. But Ethingham was never in any danger of being lost. The title remained in his family and mostly untarnished through the years. His family line was known for their acute business acumen, despite the drink. But there were other things worse than the bottle. Things like a volatile temper and a sense that they were entitled to do as they damn well pleased made life for any and all who lived within the confines of the Ethingham house an unpleasant experience.

"I have always wondered why you stayed unmarried for so long."

Lady Victoria's soft voice caused Douglas to start. When he glanced to his right, he found her patiently standing next to him and realized just how lost in his thoughts he'd become. Deciding it best to take a short break from his obsession with

Lady Cicely and her harem of admirers, he turned to face the dowager. Although, the word dowager was deceptive. It brought to mind older women, cranky with their lot in life and convinced the entire world needed to know it. At least, it did to him.

Yet, Lady Victoria would never fit into that category. Even in her fifties, she still possessed the beauty she had when she debuted. Rumor circulating amongst the ladies was that her husband, a complete and utter rake, a legend in his own right, had taken one look at her and fallen, hard. It was understandable with her fair features, blue eyes and rounded figure. She apparently had led him on a merry chase, knowing his reputation as she did. It had taken him the entire season to convince her of his intentions and his heart. Legend held true when he passed. To this day, women Douglas spoke with, those who recounted the tale, sighed when discussing Lady Victoria and her late husband.

Not comfortable with the conversation, his voice was not pleasant when he responded. "I believe most of the ton think it ill-mannered to discuss such matters, especially with a duke who rather likes to keep his private life private."

She smiled sweetly. "But when said duke is family, I believe the rules can be...stretched."

He opened his mouth to refute the assumption that every Ware had made since his relationship to Colleen had been exposed, when more laughter sounded from where Cicely stood with her enthusiasts. The crowd had grown by three or four, the men pressing closer to gain her attention. He curled his fingers into his palms and drew in a calming breath. The need to make his way through the throng and claim her as his own almost beat out his better sense. It wasn't his right to feel so possessive, but he didn't give a damn.

He eyed several of the newer attendees and ground his teeth together. Cicely would have no problem finding a man who would eagerly offer to fulfill her request. Among their nondescript faces could be the man who would taste her passion, hear her moans, be the center of her attentions.

Anger whipped through him at the thought of any of them even thinking about touching her. He looked over the crowd of gentlemen, noting their expressions, trying to remember if she had danced with any of them the other night. Was one of them the man she had planned to meet? Had she made plans for another elicit rendezvous?

"Your Grace, I believe growling at musicales is also considered ill-mannered by the ton."

He did not miss the amusement in her voice as he turned back to the older woman.

"I believe when you are a duke you are allowed to do exactly what you please." The coldness of his reply had the laughter draining from her expression and Douglas cursed himself. The words and tone were not his. They were ingrained in him, perhaps from birth, perhaps before. When he got in a temper, he had a tendency to sound like his father and grandfather. It was something he'd tried his best to hide and definitely did not act upon. But at times, his breeding reared its ugly head. "I apologize, my lady. I find myself in bad humor since listening to the performance."

Some of the color returned to her face, and her eyes softened. "That is understandable considering the performance."

A flash of red caught his eye and he glanced to see Cicely leaving behind her bevy of gentlemen. It only took a few moments for Cummings to separate himself from the others and follow her down the hall. Did women make an assignation at a musicale? Even the boldest of experienced women were more discreet.

The man had not been all that tactful about separating himself from the group. Cummings needed that generous dowry set on her and more than likely would compromise Lady Cicely to gain it. Granted, Douglas wondered why it had taken Cummings so long to act on it, but he was sure it had to do with her newly discovered assets.

"If you will excuse me, my lady, I find myself in need of fresh air."

Casting a knowing look in the direction of where he had last seen Cicely, she said, "Douglas, I know that you are...uncomfortable when we try to include you in our family." He opened his mouth to argue the point but she waved his protest away. "I see it in your reserved behavior, the way you hold yourself apart from us at gatherings. It is understandable considering your family."

Embarrassment and dread engulfed him. Not many people knew of his family's troubles, but there was no doubt that Lady Victoria had heard something. The worst of it would be if she knew the whole horrid tale of his childhood. He liked to conceal just how hellish his life had been until his grandfather had passed away after losing a duel.

"Now, do not look like that. I wanted to say that if you ever need to talk, you know Sebastian would be happy to listen."

The offer was decidedly odd. Although Victoria did take interest in her children's pursuits, she did not meddle like most mothers. To offer Sebastian as a sounding board was out of character.

When he said nothing she smiled again. "Go. I do not trust that Cummings fellow. Knowing how much money that family needs, his motives are sure to be questioned."

Douglas silently cursed when he realized that both Cummings and Cicely had been gone for several minutes. Yet at the same time, he felt his resolve reinforced. Lady Victoria was sending him on this errand. She did not approve either. Bowing his leave of Lady Victoria, Douglas hurried off to ensure that nothing nefarious happened between Cummings and Cicely.

Chapter Eight

*In which Lady Cicely discovers there is more
than music to enjoy at a musicale.*

Cicely sighed as she slowly walked to the door of the retiring room. Although excited by the attention she had received all evening, it had begun to tire her. Her mouth hurt from the plastered smile she'd worn as men spoke to her breasts. Usually men had a tendency to either ignore her completely or talk to her while eyeing other women, considering how to graciously escape being saddled with her companionship. The constant activity around her was starting to wear on her nerves, and after only one day.

She had never liked crowds, but she had been sure she would find it all so thrilling it wouldn't matter. Her list of possible prospects had dwindled in the last few hours. Every eligible candidate had made a complete and utter ass out of himself trying to vie for her regard.

And, true to her luck, the one man she craved had only tossed her dark looks all night. Despair threatened to engulf her. She had been so sure her plan was a sound one. She knew without a doubt that getting one of the men who had danced attendance on her that evening to take her up on the offer would be no problem whatsoever. But since that kiss, she wanted no one but Douglas.

"Lady Cicely."

She barely repressed the groan as she heard Cummings' voice. He approached her from behind as she faced him. Turning her back on a man with ulterior motives was never a good thing. At least he had the decency to announce himself. For some odd reason, Lady Cicely found she had no difficulty picturing the earl skulking about in some gloomy alley. She shivered slightly.

"Lord Cummings. Whatever are you doing here?" She asked the question as she donned an expression of innocence, knowing exactly why the idiot had followed her. Smiling, she hid her disgust and Cummings' grin widened. Did every man in the world think revealing her true figure made her ignorant? They acted as if she would not remember all their years of inattention.

"As if you did not know?" he said coyly.

His practiced flirting left a cold ball of frustration in her tummy. In all her years of being out in society, she had yearned for the passionate looks other women received. She had stupidly thought the games lovers played would be thrilling.

Cicely had never been so wrong in her assumptions. In one day she had gone from wallflower to Original in the eyes of the ton. She found the new role irritating. How did women like Anna take this? Not once did any of them try to engage her in interesting conversation. They talked of fashion and gossip, most of which she found as fascinating as a blank piece of paper.

When he stepped a shade too close for her comfort, she backed up. His feral smile told her he knew exactly how he was making her feel.

Another shiver snaked up her spine. "I believe you are implying that I would know your thoughts, sir. I can assure you that I do not." But she did and it was making her think twice about ever talking to the man again.

Lust flashed across his features and darkened his eyes.

Instead of the feeling of warmth Douglas' touch gave her, icy fear slithered through her. They were totally and utterly alone, and as she heard the musicians warming their instruments, she realized that any protest on her part would not be noticed. She was quite capable of being loud if the situation called for it but not quite that loud.

He crowded her against the wall, stepping so close she was aware of how the primal instinct to flee clawed at her stomach and called out a warning in her mind. Panic made her pulse throb, knowing that even if a person were to discover them before anything untoward happened, she would still be ruined.

Unaccustomed to flirtations and machinations of the ton behind closed doors and in dark corridors, she hadn't realized retiring to the privacy of a ladies' chamber alone was so dangerous. Or at least it hadn't been for her before tonight.

Cummings placed a hand on the wall beside her head, leaning closer. She tried to shrink away from him, her alarm growing as she felt his hot breath against her face. The scent of onions mingled with brandy—not to mention body odor— caused bile to rise in her throat.

As she watched him raise his free hand toward her, she knew she had to act, but something in her stayed frozen. Her mind kept screaming she should run or at the very least scream for help. But she could not do it. Her feet felt odd and heavy.

Her vision swam and a strange muted buzz sounded in her ears. It was as if she were not even there. As if she were watching from somewhere else, wondering just why she did not fight back. She closed her eyes, not wanting to watch.

"Lady Cicely."

Relief coursed through her when she heard Douglas' voice from behind Cummings. A breath she had not realized she had been holding escaped from between her lips and she opened her eyes.

Cummings, idiot that he was, slowly retreated, thinking he had set in motion his plan. Little did he know she had no intention of ruining her reputation with him. She would spend her life as an outcast before she would marry a man who kept a mistress and smelled of onions.

"Ah, you found us out, Ethingham." The self-satisfaction was barely concealed in his nasty, brandy-slurred voice.

Douglas briefly looked from Cummings to her, his eyes taking in the situation. His face was void of expression, telling her nothing of his feelings.

"Are you saying you will call on Lord Penwyth in the morning?" Douglas' voice was flat, emotionless.

There was a beat of silence. Panic raced through Cicely at the thought of what Sebastian would do to Cummings. She did not want her cousins to suffer because of her stupidity. Wanting to ensure both men understood her intentions, she stepped around Cummings and faced Douglas squarely.

"I do not believe that necessary, Your Grace."

Douglas' attention zeroed in on her as Cummings chuckled. She didn't know who she loathed more for their arrogance.

Cummings decided to take control. "Darling, Ethingham has discovered us in a most compromising situation. Your reputation will be in tatters. You truly have no choice."

His assured tone had her gnashing her teeth. Irritation had her turning around to face the offending earl. "First, I dare say he will not spread tales of this. Unlike you, he can hold his tongue. Second, just so you understand the situation, I would be happy to live out the rest of my life in a state of disgrace and die alone rather than marry someone as insulting and foul as you."

Even in the dim candlelight, she could see the color seep from his face.

"Who do you think you are?" The utter amazement in his voice had her rushing ahead without much thought.

"A woman with enough good sense to see the truth. You are beneath me."

His eyes narrowed as his lips curled into a snarl. "Your mother spread her legs for anyone with money."

Embarrassment held her immobile. What he said was true. Her mother had had a horrible standing but until this moment, no one assumed Cicely would be the same.

Years of suppressed anger started to bubble. Her own mother had mocked her about her lack of beauty and grace, and now she was having to defend her honor because of her mother's behavior.

"Perhaps you should have pursued her then."

"You little bitch." Disgust dripped from his tone as he took a step closer to her. "I should teach you a lesson." He raised his hand as if to smack her but Douglas stopped him with one sentence.

"If you will have your seconds call upon me, Cummings, I know that we can set a dawn appointment."

"What?"

Both she and Cummings yelled the question as she turned to face Douglas.

Douglas did not look at Cummings but focused his attention on her. "I told him to have his seconds call upon me."

The cold, unemotional voice did not fool her. She could feel his barely suppressed anger boiling beneath the calm surface. Those small muscles in his jaw ticked furiously. Apparently, Cummings did not realize his danger.

"I say, Ethingham. You have never been one to fight over a woman. Especially one of her ilk. A dawn appointment would be foolish, serving only to tarnish your name as well as hers."

Her stomach roiled and a new wave of bile rose in her throat. Cummings' words hit her like a physical blow. A man ready to force a woman into marriage because of his own failings was the slimiest of creatures. Even so, she knew he was right. Her mother's reputation, even before she plotted to kill Colleen, had been horrid. The fact that a bloodsucker like Cummings recognized that sent anger spiraling through her. How many years would she pay for her mother's behavior, for her father's gambling, whoring ways?

And this man, who was one of the lowest forms of society's predators, felt he had the right to judge her by her parents' actions. She wanted to spin on him, to claw his cold, bloodshot eyes out. Before she could do anything, Douglas spoke.

"I realize now that you do not understand me. You will leave here and see if you can dig up some acquaintances to act as seconds. Then we can set a meeting. But, if you do not disappear from my presence immediately, I will tear your bloody arms from your body and beat you senseless with them."

For a moment, there was no sound but the music from the hall. Cicely was stunned by the vehemence in Douglas' voice. She had known he was upset, but she'd had no idea just how furious he was. This type of anger didn't run hot, didn't have a man losing his head. This was calculated and cold and much more dangerous.

His face could have been carved out of stone. His stoic expression, the bleak, vacant look of his eyes, replaced the man she had known before. This man would not flinch at causing pain to another human.

Her heart rate accelerated. A chill wrapped itself around her core. Taking a breath hurt.

"I..." Cummings swallowed noisily. "I think—"

Irritated by his stupidity and fearing Douglas would hurt the man, Cicely spun around.

"For goodness' sake, you idiot, leave." Her voice was only a furious whisper, but his eyes widened when he comprehended the threat. Without looking at Douglas again, Cummings fled down the hall.

Cicely drew in a breath, her chest tight from the confrontation, from her worry. She smoothed her hands down the front of her dress and was surprised when they shook. It took her a few more moments to compose herself before she turned to face Douglas.

"That was completely unnecessary, Your Grace."

He studied her dispassionately before saying, "I believe it was."

Annoyed, she asked, "And why do you think you even had a right to act on my behalf?"

"Why?"

She nodded instead of answering. Otherwise she might offend him by calling him names. Her nerves were pushed to their limit. The day had been long and tiring, and while she appreciated his timing, she did not like his cold tone. After years of being an obligation, she was sick of it. She wanted something more, something he did not want to offer.

"I assumed after you practically ravished me the other night, I had the right to step in to save your reputation."

"Ravished you?" Her temper snapped. The day had been bad. The musicale had been horrible. The crowds unnerving. Cummings' insults beyond irritating, but Douglas' arrogance... "Really, Your Grace, are you sure you know what you are talking about? You did not know it was me at the time, so I had but one assumption left me."

"Really? That being?" He sounded utterly bored. As if the conversation was no more important than picking lint off his clothes.

"I assumed you allowed anonymous women to attack you."

Something shifted in his eyes, as if he came to some kind of understanding. "While I did not know it was you, you knew it was I."

Not a question but a statement. She stared at the flickering flame of a nearby wall sconce. Mortified by what he must think of her, especially now that he had found her with Cummings, she had to blink away the tears burning the backs of her eyes.

"You think I would just allow any man to touch me like that?" Her voice was a mere whisper.

"I just thought—"

"You thought I had made an assignation with another man and mistook you for him." She did not blame him. Considering that she had taunted him with her list of men, it was understandable that he would jump to that conclusion. Even comprehending his reasoning did not stop the pain. The ache in her heart almost tore it into two pieces. One side still desperately clinging to her feelings for him, the other dead or dying. It made little difference. It took every bit of control she had not to dissolve into a puddle of tears.

"Cicely—"

"No. No. Don't." She shook her head. Knowing that he apparently thought no more of her than many thought of her deceased mother—Douglas privy to the worst of it—was just the icing on top of everything else. She might not be ruined to society, but she had fallen from grace. "I understand now. I see why you think so little of me. I truly"—her voice hitched as she fought against the sob that tried to escape—"I understand."

She turned, trying to escape, to hide away from her reality. One she had created, crafted and molded into the mess it was. Like a featherbrain, she'd thought a new dress and a new hairstyle would change everything. But it had done nothing except attract the lowest forms of life.

Douglas took hold of her upper arm before she could flee.

"Come."

She was too surprised by his actions to say anything as he wandered down the hall, dragging her after him. He found a door that was unlocked and ushered her inside. Not willing to face his censure, she shook free of him and moved further into the room. It looked as if it was some sort of morning room, with its feminine design. She heard Douglas shut the door then the lock click.

"Do you want to tell me what that was all about?" He had softened his voice, but she didn't want sympathy or pity. Cicely was tired of being on the receiving end of that particular feeling.

"Why? What would it change? You've already made your assumptions."

He stood silent for some time. So long, in fact, she was afraid he would never answer. She feared hearing the key turn in the lock as he left, but it didn't come.

Finally, he spoke. "Please."

One word. Only one word, but it dissolved her defenses. "It is in actuality, quite simple. I was going to the retiring room and Cummings followed me." She shrugged, refusing to turn around and face him.

He sighed, the sound filled with irritation. "That is not what I am talking about, Cicely."

Oh, no. He wanted to talk about what had happened during the ball.

"I understand my actions tonight, and the night we...crossed paths in the library indicate just what sort of woman I am."

There was a slow beat of silence that seemed to stretch into minutes.

"And what sort of woman is that?"

Embarrassment and anger forced her to face him as she allowed the tears she had been fighting to break free. She still possessed a small amount of pride and she used it to lift her chin.

"A woman with no morals." He opened his mouth to speak, but she refused to allow him to make excuses. Reality was never very kind to her, but hiding from it these past few days had been a mistake. "Oh, what you must think of me. I originally came up with a brilliant plan to be deflowered before I am shelved. No proper lady formulates a plan to lose her virginity." She hiccupped. "And then you found me tonight in the company of the vilest sort of hanger-on. Well, I am sure you thought the worst."

"The worst?"

She blinked repeatedly, confusion jumping into the muddle of feelings coursing through her. He had leaned against the doors, his face hidden in the shadows, so she had no idea what kind of expression he held. Was this the cold stranger who had threatened to kill Cummings without a thought? Or was this the man she knew, the one she had fallen in love with?

Angrily, she brushed the tears from her cheeks. "Seriously, Douglas, it does not take a highly intelligent woman to understand what I now look like, or what I apparently am. Perhaps Cummings was correct in stating the apple does not fall far from the tree." Somewhere in the back of her mind, she knew her voice was tinged with hysteria. Trying to calm herself, she drew in a shuddering breath and continued on. "I would have never guessed I was like my mother, but, true to form, I attract the lowest type of men."

Again, he waited to speak, as if weighing what she said. With her emotions running wild and her senses all but overloaded, she resented his cool headedness.

"You liked what Cummings was doing?"

She shuddered as her skin prickled at the memory. The blood rushed from her head. Her stomach churned. "Good God, no. It was everything I could do not to vomit in his face." Needing to move, she walked to a small end table with curio pieces set about in display. After a moment, she continued, her voice flat. "My mother was right, and why I listened to my cousin and aunt I do not know. My mother told me what would happen."

He moved away from the door, walking slowly toward her. "What did your mother say?"

"She told me exactly what kind of man would find me attractive. The saddest part of this is that until tonight, no man has found me even remotely pretty."

"That is not true."

His defense of her caused another wave of tears to pour out. With Douglas' reputation as a rake, no one would ever guess he was honorable, but he was. He had saved her reputation, and now he was trying to soothe her worries. And he did it for no other reason than his own honor.

"Yes, it is. I cannot believe I even thought I could attract a man worth anything."

"Cicely, please—"

"No." She backed away as he moved closer.

He stopped and his eyes flashed with worry. "Darling, you are wrong."

"About what?" she asked, sniffing loudly as her nose had now started to run. Where had she tucked that handkerchief? "The fact that my mother had the worst of reputations? Maybe that I thought a new dress would change everything? Or that only disgusting lechers are attracted to me? And when I say me, please rest assured I know it has nothing to do with me and only to do with the dowry Sebastian has graciously placed for me and my bosom."

He frowned. "None of that. I know of one particular gentleman who found you attractive before you changed your look."

That caught her attention. She knew of no one remotely interested. Assuming he was fibbing to make her feel better, she asked, "And who would that be? Point me in his direction and you will be free of the obligation of protecting me. If there were such a man, perhaps he will accept me regardless of my family history and this whole foolish charade can be over."

He crossed his arms over his chest.

"I mean it, Your Grace. You tell me who he is and I will find a way to pursue him. As they say at the track 'have at it'."

"Have at it?" His lips curved and his voice dipped. "What a particularly wonderful idea."

Gone was the cold, emotionless aristocrat. In his place was the consummate rake. Even being the novice that she was, she had heard the seduction in his voice, knew what it meant. Every thought in her brain dissolved as he drew near. Heat raced along her nerve endings. She did nothing but watch him approach. Unable to tear her gaze from his, she realized that she was frozen again, but unlike earlier with Cummings, there was no fear involved. This time her heart skipped a beat as her body warmed. With each step he took, she felt her temperature rise, her senses thrill.

"I have to say, Cicely, oddly enough, I completely agree with that plan."

He stepped so close, she felt his legs brush against the silk skirts of her dress. The spicy scent of him surrounded her. She licked her lips which had suddenly gone dry. When she looked up at him, the unabashed arousal darkening his features had Cicely curling her toes within her slippers.

"What plan would that be?"

The corner of his mouth kicked up—as did her heart rate. "The charade being over. I agree with it and…"

She swallowed, her skin prickling with anticipation. "And?"

"I would like to have at it."

With that statement, he slid his arms around her waist, pulled her tightly against him, and bent his head to press his mouth against hers. Without a thought, she slipped her hands up his chest and behind his neck. Even through their layers of clothing she could feel his body molded against hers. He raised one hand to cup her jaw, his fingers skimming over her skin. Blood rushed from her head, leaving it spinning.

He murmured something against her lips, something she could not comprehend, but it did not matter. Because, in the next instant, he flicked his tongue over the seam of her lips and she melted.

Chapter Nine

In which a duke loses more than his head.

Douglas felt Cicely concede and open her mouth for him. He stole inside, reveling in the sweet, tangy taste. It flowed through his body, warmed his blood. She pressed closer, those magnificent breasts flattened against his chest.

She moaned his name. The delicious sound hurtled him back into the memories of that night they had accidentally kissed. The touches, the tastes, having her on his lap, feeling the feminine heat of her through his trousers.

Knowing that it would go too far, that he could not risk her reputation because he couldn't control his baser urges, with much regret he broke the kiss. Both of them were breathing heavily, their hearts beating against each other.

"Oh, my."

The deepening of her voice had him leaning in to steal another quick kiss, but he found himself lingering. While he cupped the back of her head with one hand, he moved the other to her breast. The delicate fabric gave way easily to his questing fingers. He brushed his thumb over her nipple, thrilling him as it hardened into a tight nub. Wanting a sample, Douglas kissed a path down the soft skin of her neck to her exposed breast.

In the dim light, he could not see well enough. He wanted, no, needed to see. He slipped an arm to her waist and spun them around so he could lay her on the sofa. With a shaft of moonlight spilling across her bare breasts, his breath caught in his throat. Full, rounded and with the sweetest pink nipples he had ever seen. Heat seared a path to his groin, and his cock twitched at the sight.

"Douglas." The worry in her voice had him snatching his gaze from her bosom and moving to her face. Apprehension shone in her eyes. The sight melted his heart. *Such an innocent.* She had no idea just how close the barbarian in him was to tearing off her clothes and taking her right there.

"Yes, love?"

She sighed, which in turn had his gaze moving to her breasts. "I know you may be old hat with this sort of thing, but I am not." She paused and sighed again, as if trying to gather courage. "It is a tiny bit disconcerting to lay here with my bosom bared and you staring at it."

Little did she know that he would be happy to strip off every bit of his clothing and allow her to look her fill. Unfortunately that would not do since even now her reputation was at stake. But also because he knew, no matter how brave she portrayed herself, there was a good chance she would go running in the opposite direction.

Beneath her humor he detected something else, an emotion he could not ignore. The vulnerability he witnessed in her soft brown eyes struck him to the core. He had never pegged her as being particularly defenseless, but in this she was. One wrong word from him would crush her.

The need to soothe her worries engulfed him. Not until that moment had he realized just how much he wanted to be the one who made her happy. Trying to gather his thoughts, he smoothed one of her eyebrows, then the other. The heat in his blood shifted, deepened, evolved into a sentiment he did not want to acknowledge.

And because of that, because being with her meant more, he forced himself to move away. It cost him, more than she would ever know, but he said, "I apologize, Cicely. I know that you..."

He couldn't continue because his gaze had drifted to her breasts again. Her nipples were still hard, almost calling out to be touched, tasted...

His body threatened to revolt against his better judgment. There was no way he could concentrate with her chest bared like that. With much regret, he pulled the delicate fabric back over her bosom, mourning the loss.

"What is the matter?"

The pain he heard in her voice caught his heart unaware. Women had always come easy to him, but this one, this one could hurt him. Just hearing her worry, knowing that her pain affected him this way, made him feel exposed. He wanted to lash out, to protect himself from harm, until he glanced at her face again. Unshed tears glistened in her eyes and a touch of the self-recrimination he had witnessed earlier shone in them.

Inwardly, he groaned as an ache stung his heart. He had brought her to this. She would see it as another rejection, he knew that. And it was not, far from it. His mind was still whirling with the revelation. Telling her could result in rejection, or worse, her knowledge of his feelings could be used to control him. She was not looking for marriage. Her only goal was to learn the ways of love.

Ahh, that was it. She wanted to learn how to love, and he could teach her that. Lessons in seduction and in the process tie her to him with lust.

"I have decided to grant your request."

She said nothing and he found himself worrying she had changed her mind. She pulled herself up to her elbows and studied him.

"My request?" Her voice sounded strained but he did not detect any change in her expression.

"Your request for...lessons."

Something came and went in her eyes, something close to regret, but it was gone before he could detect exactly what it was. She pursed her lips in thought.

"Then, you would teach me everything I want to know?" Excitement had deepened her tone.

He swallowed. "Yes."

Before he went against his better judgment and did just that, he shifted further away from the sofa. And temptation. He turned from her, toward the desk and the window. Looking out over the gardens, he told his body she was not asking for everything now, it would not be right.

She was silent again for a moment. The crunch of leather told him she had risen and he sensed her coming near.

"No objections, you will be thorough?"

Thorough? The innocent that she was, she had no idea just how much and how detailed he wanted to be. He could just imagine bringing her to her first peak, hearing her moan...

Her fingers brushed along his jaw. With a steady hand and a firm grip, she turned him to face her. The sight of her, moonlight streaming through the window, her hair mussed, her lips swollen from his kisses and her expression earnest, almost had him forgetting his plan. *Bloody hell.* His breathing deepened, his body hardened. She looked delightful in this condition and it had his mind thinking of other ways to view her. Like naked.

Damnit to hell. If he did not get both of them back to a public area soon, he would take her virginity without a thought. He lifted his hand and wrapped it around her wrist. Her eyes widened then dilated as he pressed her fingers to his mouth. They trembled slightly as he flicked his tongue out over the tip of her index finger.

"I want to teach you everything." He gave her one more kiss, this time on her palm before he let go of her wrist. "But not tonight." Cicely opened her mouth to argue—of course she did—but he plowed ahead. "You have just been through a horrible experience with Cummings. Not to mention, we have been gone for too long, and while you apparently have no problem playing ducks and drakes with your reputation, I will not allow it."

She frowned at that. "So when?"

Her eagerness had him chuckling. "Soon."

"But—"

"Do not worry, love. I will take care of everything. You did ask for lessons. I happen to know how to conduct an affair."

She nodded, a small smile curving her lips. "Of course, Your Grace."

"First order of business. When we are alone, please call me Douglas."

"Yes, I guess that would be best."

A delightful laugh slipped from her as she raised her hands to work over her mussed hair. The simple act held him mesmerized while her fingers worked to get out some of the worst of the tangles. There was something so intimate about watching her do this. Already aroused, he found himself getting even harder and it made him feel like a voyeur. What was worse, the action brought her breasts up and over the low bodice of her dress. He was sure that at any moment she would come spilling out of it and he would be lost. There would be no way to control his lustful instincts if he saw her breasts again. Unfortunately, she had her hair arranged within moments and lowered her arms.

"I guess we should be getting back."

Shaking himself free of the fantasy of having her do the same thing in front of him, but naked, Douglas cleared his throat.

"I think you should go first. It will not be noticeable if you walk out alone, but if we show up together it will cause a stir. You slip in. I will wait until the next performance is over."

"It is not very gentlemanly of you to subject me to another bad performance. I think you should be the one to suffer."

Knowing just what she had been through that evening, he could not help but admire her ability to find humor in the situation. For that, and a whole lot more, he leaned forward and gave her a quick kiss. As he pulled away, surprise lit her features.

"Now, off with you."

He escorted her to the door and watched as she opened it, leaning out to check the hallway. With a small smile tossed over her shoulder, she hastened through the doorway. It was not until he heard the click of the tumbler falling into place that he allowed a breath he had not known he was holding loose. Closing his eyes, he scrubbed his hand over his face.

The woman was going to drive him insane. Correction, she already had. She never did one thing he expected. Well, she had before her request for lessons. From that point on she had him twisting one way and the other, trying to figure out what she would do next. He was sure that before he got her to the altar, she would lead him on a merry chase. That one thought stopped him—astounded him. He waited for the revulsion, for the abject horror that the prospect of marriage usually caused. As he turned the idea over in his mind, the rightness of it settled in his heart. Never before had one woman seemed so perfect for him, but he had his work cut out for him. She was adamant against marriage—or so she said. It wasn't as if he thought she was trying to trap him, far from it. She offered up her virginity without hesitation, as if it meant little to nothing to her. But in this, he knew she was pretending.

That made him pause. She thought she would never marry because she could not garner an offer. But that theory was blown out of the water today. So what else made her think she was unsuitable? Granted, she worried about her mother's and father's reputation, but that did not seem to stop that bastard Cummings. The rage he had banked for Cicely roared to life again. The damn bugger was the vilest of creatures. And there would probably be more just like him. With her looks so readily visible, and that monstrous dowry Sebastian had put on her, she would be pursued. He could solve that problem by offering for her right now, but he understood Cicely would turn him down flat.

That brought him back to why she would not marry. Granted, having a mother go mad and plot to kill family would probably not recommend you to most gentlemen. But with his background... He snorted. Well, her family upbringing was a walk in the park compared to his relatives. He understood hiding the true nature of your familial relations. It was one thing he guarded, the one thing that he never wanted to tell another living soul and the reason he had planned on never marrying.

Sighing, he walked to the door and entered the hall. The off-key screeching of the soprano who had tortured them in the first set made him cringe then smile, thinking of Cicely's comment earlier. He paused in front of a small mirror in the hall. After righting his appearance, he headed to the ballroom and Cicely.

Just as he reached the arched doorway, the singing—and that was a very liberal use of the word—stopped. Studying the crowd, he looked for Cummings and was pleased to see the man had apparently taken his advice and fled. Still, he needed to have a chat with Ware, just to make sure he knew the risk and to ask him to be a second.

Douglas' attention moved on to the woman who had become an obsession. She was chatting with her cousin Anna. Something the younger woman said caused Cicely to smile and Douglas responded in kind.

"One of these days, you will put yourself out of your misery."

He looked to his left and found that Bridgerton had slipped up beside him.

"You talk in riddles, Bridgerton. Cut line."

"You are as bad as Sebastian was with Colleen."

Douglas, knowing that was not far from the truth, decided to ignore the remark.

"I did not notice you earlier," Douglas stated.

The smile on the older man's face faded. "I had one or two things to look over before I could make it." The tone of Bridgerton's voice did not invite comment.

"And you rushed here in musical appreciation," Douglas said.

For a few moments, Bridgerton did not answer. His interest was centered on a cluster of people who had gathered around Anna and Cicely. Without moving his gaze away, he said, "Of course."

"It could not be something—or should I say someone—else that brought you around?"

Bridgerton slowly turned and gave Douglas his attention. He offered Douglas a mocking smile.

"You could be right about that, old chap. If so, I am worse than both you and Ware." Something over Douglas' shoulder caught Bridgerton's interest. "I'll leave you to your pursuit, Your Grace."

Douglas caught his arm as he passed by. "Come by Ware's in the morning. I have something I need to discuss with you both."

Bridgerton's gaze turned speculative, but he said nothing, just nodded before moving on. He headed straight for Catherine, who Douglas had not seen earlier either, and masterfully maneuvered to her side. He was a little flummoxed to find that Bridgerton and one of his own paramours had a connection.

A bubble of laughter erupted across the room, drawing his notice back to Cicely. She was laughing, the sound hard to hear above the din of conversation. But he could still detect the joy in it, see the excitement on her face and the sparkle in her eyes.

Something warm wound into his heart. When had her happiness become so important to him? It had never been like this with a woman, as if her very pleasure was his duty. Even as he tried to deny it, the feeling expanded, burning his chest. He rubbed his palm over the pain. He knew what it meant, what it could mean to his peace of mind. Surely somewhere in hell his forefathers cackled in delight as Douglas admitted to himself he was in love with the impossible woman.

Chapter Ten

In which Lady Cicely gloats, if only to herself.

Cicely snuggled deeper beneath her crisp bed linens, refusing to acknowledge the coming of morning. She didn't want to rise, not yet. Her dreams were just too delicious to abandon. But Betsy apparently did not know of her decision to sleep the day away. Either that or she did not appreciate the depth of the desire.

"You missed breakfast, my lady."

She said this in an impossibly cheery voice, right before she ripped open the heavy floral curtains, baring the room to the bright ravages of an unclouded sun. Cicely groaned and pulled her pillow over her face.

"My lady?"

The worry in Betsy's voice made Cicely grimace. She was not usually a layabout but after all the excitement of yesterday, it felt like the most wonderful thing in the world to do. The only thing lacking was Douglas next to her. That thought brought forth a rush of goose bumps that rose on her flesh as she indulged in her fantasy. Cuddling close to him, the heat of him warming her...

"Lady Cicely, do I need to call on Lady Victoria or Lady Colleen? Lady Victoria asked about you after you had to leave the musicale."

Sighing at the loss of her delicious fantasy—not to mention her privacy—she pushed her pillow aside and sat up. Against the onslaught of sunshine, she had to squint to see anything. She rubbed at the sleep in her eyes and yawned.

"No, I'm fine now."

Betsy stood near the windows watching her with apprehension. "I'm not so sure. Are you certain?"

Cicely was too tired to deal with this, but she also didn't want to answer numerous questions, and she did not want to hurt Betsy's feelings. "I swear I am fine. I think the excitement of the evening, the heat of the room, all of it just didn't settle well with me. I'm still a girl who prefers the quieter entertainments. I find the crush quite..." She searched for the right word. "Overwhelming."

Betsy smiled and went about the room, getting things ready for Cicely's morning bath. "I told Lady Victoria that was all there was to it."

Of course. Betsy was never wrong, thought Cicely with a smile. There was a knock at the door heralding the footmen with her bath. The next few minutes were spent getting the bath ready for her. After they left, Cicely slid off her bed.

She stretched her arms over her head while Betsy poured the lavender-scented salts into the steaming water. Cicely had slept like a dead weight, but it had not been restful. Her dreams had been filled with a mixture of Douglas and the horrible altercation with Cummings. It was such a strange and confusing combination of emotions that her sleep had not afforded her the respite she needed. Her stomach growled, which caused Betsy and Cicely to laugh.

"I'll have them fix you a tray and bring it up."

"Give me at least half an hour. I feel the need to indulge this morning."

Grinning, Betsy nodded before slipping out the door to leave Cicely alone with her thoughts. As she disrobed, the memories of the night before brought a smile to her lips. Her hands traced places on her skin he had touched and the nerve endings flared to life once again. She knew what Douglas had shown her had been but a drop in the bucket of his knowledge of lovemaking. She shivered. She could not wait until their first lesson.

Stepping into the scented water and sinking down, she closed her eyes. Although the sunlight didn't hurt so badly anymore, Cicely wanted nothing more than to pamper herself, escape into her fantasy. As the aroma of lavender surrounded her, the hotness of the water relaxed her muscles.

She only had one worry and that was Douglas' decision regarding Cummings. Cicely frowned over her thoughts as she opened her eyes and picked up her soap. Lathering it, she contemplated a way to get Douglas to abandon the idea of a duel. She was sure without a doubt he would win, but there was always a chance he would not. Not to mention, there could be retribution from the crown for holding a duel. Douglas held a lot of power due to his title, but there was only so much Prinny would allow.

Cicely could not bear him putting his life and his good name at risk because of her stupidity. It was not her fault that Cummings was a nasty man. Still, she should have been smarter about where she was going and who was following. She would not have Douglas pay for her mistake.

She scrubbed a dripping hand over her face.

Somehow, she had to get him to rescind his offer. If she knew him, and she did, he would end up here to talk to Sebastian about it. There was no way possible for her to handle it if Douglas was put in danger because of her. Although she would never admit it to him, she loved him. He looked at her and her heart leaped. He touched her and she melted.

Douglas did not feel what she did. Oh, he was attracted to her. He proved that much last night. But what she felt went beyond attraction, beyond lust. There had been a void in her life. For many years, she felt as if she stood on the fringes of society. Her childhood had not been the most pleasant experience. True, she did not know about the mass amount of her mother's liaisons until after she had died. Still, her mother had spent every day of Cicely's childhood pecking away at her fragile confidence. Prudence Ware never understood Cicely's fascination with history. She had let her daughter know on more than one occasion what an oddity she was. And with a father who barely registered the existence of his daughter, her childhood had been lonely.

Her cousins and aunt had filled part of that void after her mother's death. But something had been missing, something she found with Douglas. When she was with him, she forgot to worry about her appearance. She could just be Cicely and she knew he did not care.

Her stomach growled again. She had been so nervous before her appearance at the musicale she had eaten little yesterday and now was paying the price.

By the time Betsy arrived, Cicely was already in her robe, sitting in her favorite chair, reading the diary and its cryptic messages, awaiting her food. A tray laden with toast, chocolate, coddled eggs and kidney beans made her mouth water.

"Oh, Betsy, this looks wonderful!" She laid down the diary, careful of the delicate pages.

"Thank you, my lady. I will make sure Cook knows it. Now don't dawdle."

Cicely sipped her chocolate with relish. She savored the warm liquid. A hint of flavor lingered on her lips as she set the cup down, picked up her fork and applied herself to her breakfast.

"Do my aunt or cousin have plans today?"

"No, I believe they arranged for a day in. Visitors. After the excitement of last night coupled with the plans for attending the Merryweather Ball, both ladies are quite occupied." Betsy busied herself at Cicely's dresser, pulling frilly undergarments out with a flourish. "What I mean to say is that the duke and the earl are downstairs. I thought you would like to make an appearance."

For a brief moment, Cicely was sure she had heard Betsy incorrectly. But when she processed the words, she said, "Ethingham?"

Betsy shot her a knowing look. "Yes, and Earl Bridgerton. They both arrived about ten minutes ago. Looked quite dashing, set for business, and perhaps a little annoyed. Requested an audience with your cousin."

Her mind was still whirling with the implications of his arrival so she did not think before she asked, "Why would Ethingham want to meet with Anna?"

Chuckling, Betsy hurried over to Cicely's side. "Last night definitely addled your senses. Not Lady Anna. Lord Penwyth. Showed up here, dressed to the nines, he did, requesting to see him." She paused. "Demanded. He demanded an audience. The lord came immediately and they have been in the study for about ten minutes along with the Earl of Bridgerton."

Worry had Cicely frowning. Why would Douglas want to speak with Sebastian? Her thoughts earlier about the duel and seconds had her jumping out of the chair.

"I want to wear the new blue morning dress."

For once holding her tongue, Betsy smiled and did Cicely's bidding.

Cicely calmed her breathing, hoping to avert disaster. If Douglas asked Sebastian to be his second that would end all chances of her talking him out of it. That Bridgerton was here did not bode well for her plans. She'd known he would approach Sebastian, but she'd had no idea he would make it here so early.

She did not care what she needed to do, but one way or another, she would make sure Douglas did not make that dawn appointment.

CS80

Douglas studied his cousin's husband, who was taking in everything he had told him and Bridgerton of Cicely's encounter with Cummings the night before.

"And you say he frightened her?" The nasty edge to Penwyth's voice caused Douglas to relax. He did not doubt Sebastian cared for Cicely, but many men would wonder if she'd led Cummings on.

"I heard more of the conversation than Lady Cicely believes. I saw her face." He shook his head. "He planned on going past frightening her. I believe if I had not found them and interrupted, he might have succeeded in doing more than just compromising her."

"The man has no morals," Bridgerton remarked. "I have heard he is a regular visitor to the House of Rod. Seems sadist tendencies do not skip a generation in that family, as his father was a customer also."

Sebastian's eyes widened at that. "Who would have thought that of the little bastard?" His tone dripped with disgust. "I have a feeling I know what particular vice he goes there to fill."

"What do you need from us?" Bridgerton asked.

"Seconds," Douglas said.

A muscle flexed in Penwyth's cheek, and his gaze drifted to the fire. "You challenged him?"

Douglas shrugged. "I had no choice."

Without moving his attention from the blaze, Sebastian nodded. "I knew I should have attended last night, but with going out to the Merryweather Ball tonight, well, Colleen and I hate to be gone two nights in a row." He glanced at Bridgerton, then settled his gaze on Douglas. His piercing blue eyes sharpened with irritation. "Have you heard from his seconds?"

"No. I believe today that we will find the knocker removed from the door and a notice that he has left for the country. Or better yet, the continent."

The earl sighed. "I find myself in your debt again."

Penwyth appeared older. Having four women in the house was bound to do that to a man. All of the responsibility. That on top of his duties to title and estate and those of being a new father.

Douglas smiled, remembering how the earl had hated the fact he had been the one to find Colleen when she had been pushed down the stairs. At the time, no one but Douglas knew of his familial connection to Colleen.

"Well, old man, how about my pick of that prime horseflesh you have on the estate?"

He snorted. "I think not. Besides, Anna is in charge of the stables. For all her girlish ways, she is still horse mad. With the children, the estate, not to mention my wife, I welcome the help."

A grunt sounded from Bridgerton, who was now the one gazing broodingly at the fire. "Fat chance there. That chit would not part with one of her stable."

"You would know," Penwyth remarked.

With a dark glance in his friend's direction, Bridgerton said, "You can depend on us for anything in that regard. I cannot stand Cummings, could not before this."

All humor fled Sebastian's face. "You can count on it, Your Grace. The one thing we need to ensure is that my wife, mother and sister do not find out about this. Colleen would have a fit."

Douglas chuckled to cover the envy piercing his heart. He begrudged his friend nothing, especially knowing that Penwyth had almost lost Colleen. Still, witnessing their happy life stung. Jealousy of a married couple was a new and uncomfortable feeling for Douglas. Up until last night, he thought never to marry. His parents' marriage had left him wary of the institution.

The argument had been made by distant and not-so-distant cousins that he should marry and produce heirs. He'd felt no rush since he had a few cousins who had a multitude of offspring. Of course, that changed the night Cicely had kissed him. After that kiss, there was no going back, no switching course. She would be his...that was not a doubt. Knowing her own revulsion to the institution of marriage, Douglas decided the only way to change her mind would be through those lessons.

"Nothing sadder than a henpecked husband." Bridgerton's amused voice brought Douglas out of his dismal plans.

The smile returned to Sebastian's face. "Ah, you should be so lucky, Daniel. Find yourself a good woman. Settle down. That is the true way to happiness." Voices sounded outside the room. "And happiness is about to intrude."

Douglas nodded and stood as Sebastian and Daniel rose from their chairs. With an explosion of both sound and force, the door burst inward. Anna led the pack. Behind her came Colleen carrying Charles.

"I see that my family has decided to afford me privacy as usual," Penwyth said but there was only warmth in his voice.

"Oh, pooh, Sebastian." This came from Anna, who smiled at Douglas and Bridgerton as she hurried around the desk to give her brother a quick peck on the cheek. "Fitzgerald said Douglas was here and he said his name in front of old Charlie here."

Sebastian's sigh was long and dramatic. "Anna, I have asked you not to call your nephew Charlie."

"As I said before, pooh."

"Anna, quit trying to start a fight with Sebastian," Colleen admonished. "Douglas. Daniel. It is so nice to see you both this morning."

Leaning forward, she brushed her lips against Douglas' cheek. Even after two years, the action took him by surprise. Open displays of love were a new and different experience for him. The Wares seemed to not think twice about showing affection, something that had been disdained in his own household. Douglas had grown up in such a sterile environment. No one touched anything, least of all each other. It was unheard of.

When Colleen pulled away, Charles leaned toward Douglas and he had no choice but to take the toddler from his mother. It was that or watch the pleasantly plump little boy plummet to the ground.

"You just saw Douglas last night." This came from her husband.

Colleen gave him a glare then moved onto Daniel, affording him the same attention she had given Douglas. "I am going to have to quote Anna here and say, pooh."

Douglas barely noticed the byplay between the couple as Charles stared up at him. The deep blue Ware eyes studied him as if Douglas had the secrets of life and with an expectation that Douglas would share those secrets. The thought of having his own children, children both he and Cicely would share, tugged at his heart. Thinking he would not be a good role model for children, Douglas had not contemplated fatherhood. He'd had not one good example of how a loving father should act, at least while growing up. But now, now he wanted those children and he wanted them with Cicely.

The object of his thoughts rushed into the room. She came to an abrupt halt just inside the door, her eyes widening almost comically at the crowd gathered there. Embarrassment flushed her face. She was breathing heavily, as if she had exerted a great amount of work to get to the study.

Sighing, he shifted his weight, trying to ease the heaviness in his loins. Young Charles was good cover for his distress. The woman had him weaving between so many opposing emotions, Douglas was amazed he could think straight.

"I can explain everything, Sebastian."

Utter silence greeted that announcement. No one seemed to know what to say to that. Even Charles stopped his chatter.

Douglas froze.

Her cousin shook free of his surprise more quickly than the rest of the group and broke the silence.

With a smile, Sebastian asked, "Why don't you explain all of it to us?"

Chapter Eleven

In which Lady Cicely must clarify.

Cicely swallowed her nerves and faced her cousin. Not many people would take in a poor relation, especially one with a mother who had plotted to kill you and your wife. But Sebastian had done that and more. He had given her a family, somewhere to belong. She did not want to disappoint him. She shot a glare in Douglas' direction—who stared at her expectantly—and then moved her attention back to Sebastian.

"Do you want to explain what you are talking about, Cicely?" Sebastian smiled at her, a kind light in his blue eyes that made her feel even worse.

She glanced at Douglas and realized with a start that he was holding Charles. Unfortunately the image of Douglas holding a young toddler was entirely too enticing. It reminded her faintly of her earlier dreams. She did not think she had dreamt of having the duke's heir, but the process of acquiring one... Flustered, she turned in the direction of her cousin once again.

When she found Sebastian studying her and then flashing a concerned frown at Douglas, her worry increased tenfold.

"Colleen, could you take my meddlesome sister"—to which said sister huffed and mumbled something that sounded remarkably like pooh—"and our son and let me have a word with Douglas, Daniel and Cicely alone?"

Although Anna complained loudly, Colleen ushered her out. On her way she stopped in front of Douglas and recaptured her small son, who protested even more loudly than Anna. His wails echoed a retreat out in the marble hallway. A smartly liveried footman closed the heavy doors, leaving Sebastian, Cicely, Daniel and Douglas sequestered in a beat of uncomfortable silence.

"Do have a seat, everyone."

Cicely and Douglas settled into the matching boxwood and ebony George III chairs that faced Sebastian's desk as Daniel sat on the settee.

"Cicely, first you must understand that this situation calls for some sort of action. I know that is a concept both offending and foreign to you, however, it is one you simply must accept given the circumstance."

She frowned, her thoughts turning decidedly ominous. Damn Douglas and his blasted honor. She licked her lips. The idea he would risk his life...

Cicely said, "I do not see why my opinion could not at the very least be considered. It does involve me."

Sebastian looked at Douglas as if waiting for him to intervene and when he realized he would have no help from that quarter, said, "These...situations are best handled by men. It would not do for you to be..." He seemed to hesitate as he searched for the word he wanted. "Sullied."

"*Sullied?*" Is that how Douglas saw her? Is that why he agreed to her lessons? Anger had her jumping out of her chair. "And just why is it, Cousin, that men get to decide? This directly affects me and I want to know why I do not get a voice in the matter."

"Cicely," Sebastian sighed.

"You have accepted me here, most graciously—"

"Cicely—"

"But I do not think that you need to concern yourself with this nonsense at all."

"Cicely!" Sebastian barked.

She snapped her mouth shut.

Using two fingers at each temple, he rubbed in slow, small circles. He had dark crescents under his eyes, making her wonder if it was recreation, her nephew, niece or some business trouble that had kept Sebastian from a full night's sleep. Guilt held her tongue.

"You are just as stubborn as my wife. This is a matter of not only your honor, but the duke's as well. Douglas had to challenge Cummings and that is the end of it."

"It's good to know I have so many looking out for *my* honor."

"Had I been in Douglas' shoes, I, too, would have challenged the bas—rake," Bridgerton said.

She shot him a look of irritation, which was met with a smile. "There really is no need for this. Cummings is afraid of what His Grace will do to him, and as Douglas said last night, there is a good chance the bounder is gone."

"Cicely, there is no guarantee that he has left," Sebastian insisted. "He did what had to be done and I am forever in his debt for being there for you."

While she appreciated his support and protection, she could not stand for this. "It was my fault for being alone and not being aware of my surroundings. And while it was not the most pleasant experience, I daresay I will survive. There is no need for His Grace to risk his life."

"I told you, Lady Cicely, it was not your fault." Just the sound of Douglas' gentle tone had heat curling in her tummy. She chanced a glance in his direction and found herself melting under his regard. His thick hair fell a bit haphazardly onto his forehead. It only increased his charm. His lips, lips that had only last night conveyed warmth and tenderness, twitched with amusement. "Men like Cummings are not fit for company and the sooner he leaves, whether by carriage or by bullet, the better for everyone."

She offered Douglas a tentative smile and the air between them thickened as detailed memories of the night before flashed through her mind. Heat flushed her face as she realized from his look that he was remembering the same thing.

Sebastian cleared his throat, breaking the spell. When she could tear her gaze away from Douglas, she faced her cousin and had to fight a grimace at his dark expression.

She decided to press her point. "I do not approve of the duel."

"I do not care."

The thread of irritation was evident in Sebastian's voice. For all she loved about her cousin, when he made up his mind, there was little one could do to change it. Knowing that, and understanding that arguing with him would get her nowhere, Cicely thought it best to retreat and regroup before confronting either man again.

Sebastian moved several papers on his desk, stacking them in a neat pile. "Being the coward that he is, I have a feeling Cummings will not show to face Douglas. Even so, I do not want you revealing this to Colleen and especially not to Anna. That girl cannot keep a single, blessed thing to herself."

Bridgerton snorted. "That is putting it mildly. There is not a secret she could hold for more than a minute."

Sebastian did not even look at his friend. Instead, his gaze bore into Cicely. "Are we in agreement about Colleen and Anna?"

She nodded. "What do you propose we tell them we were all discussing? Anna will pounce on me the moment I leave."

All three men were silent. Sebastian grimaced.

"History?" Douglas ventured.

That would certainly put Anna off, even if she poked and prodded. Cicely began speaking of tomes and studies and Anna switched off, surveying the room for fabric samples.

"Wise choice." Amusement threaded Bridgerton's tone.

"Still," Sebastian said. "I am the earl and the head of this household. Tell them history if you must but I'd rather you just say you cannot talk about it."

Deciding there was no arguing with them, and needing time to think, she stood to leave. "Very well. If you gentlemen will excuse me, I need to make it out before the streets are too crowded."

"Out?" They said in unison.

She smiled sweetly. "Yes. Out."

As she slipped into the hallway, Anna, true to her prediction, leapt on her, pulling her away from Sebastian's study and into the formal greeting room. "What was that all about?"

"I cannot say."

Anna frowned. "Cannot or will not?"

"Cannot. Earl decree backed by ducal threat. In a manner of speaking. There is nothing really to worry about."

"I was not worried. I just wanted to know. I had not thought to be worried. Should I be worried?"

"No."

"Very well, then I just want to know."

Cicely laughed and offered Anna a hug. When she pulled back, Anna was staring at her curiously. It was then that she realized this was the first time she had offered affection openly.

To cover her embarrassment, Cicely said, "Really, it was nothing. They had a historical question that I, with my contacts at the society, might be able to help them with."

"Oh." Anna's eyes glassed over as Cicely expected.

"Do you want to go with me to the lending library?"

Anna shook her head. A smile tugged up the corner of her mouth. "No. Dewhurst is stopping by for a ride in the park."

"Betsy said everyone was staying in today."

Anna laughed. "That had been the plan but he sent over a note requesting a ride in the park. Why don't you come with me?"

"No, I need to get to the library. And, if the house is quiet, I can spend some more time looking over the diary. I started in again this morning, but, well..."

Anna nodded then leaned close, brushing her lips over Cicely's cheek. "I will see you later."

She watched Anna scamper off to ready herself for the ride with her new beau and Cicely could not help but feel a bit envious. Even at Anna's age, Cicely had experienced no carefree courting, rides in the park or flowers the morning after balls.

Shaking off her morose memories, Cicely ascended the stairs to her room. She needed a day out doing something she loved, something she coveted. Balls, courting and whatnot would just have to wait.

CR80

"Is there something I should know about?"

Sebastian's voice cut through the silence threatening to strangle Douglas since Cicely had left.

He turned the heavy gilded book over in his hand, examining the structural binding. Whoever had originally bound the book had taken great care in his work. Douglas admired the craftsmanship. "No. Why do you ask?"

Sebastian paused, studying him, assessing him. Douglas hated the feeling because it brought back memories of being called into his father's study, being reprimanded, and the lashes that always followed. His throat closed, choking him. He looked for Sebastian's decanter. A good swill would help.

"Colleen noticed your regard last night."

He returned the book to its precise position on the shelf and helped himself to a small one-finger pull. "My regard?"

"You seemed to be paying particularly close attention to Cicely before you left for the musicale. I am wondering now if she had the right of it. There is something between you two."

He examined the weighty cut crystal. The light refracted from the sharp, cut angles, the amber liquid inside adding to the effect. "Indeed."

"Is there something we should discuss?"

"Other than how she finds me pompous and overbearing? Or perhaps how she does not care for my meddling in her affairs?" The word affairs almost choked him. He quickly took a swallow to cover.

Sebastian remained unmoved. "No. Not those things."

Douglas opened his mouth to deny it again, but decided against it. It wasn't time to speak of his intentions. "Not as of yet."

"But you foresee the possibility of a reason to in the future?"

Douglas nodded, once.

"Well, then I believe that is all we have to say."

CʒꙄꙄ

Colleen let herself into Sebastian's study, determined to get to the bottom of whatever was going on with her cousin. Before he left, Douglas had said little, evading her questions with a smile and promise to meet them at the theater later in the evening. Bridgerton told her to mind her own business.

Still, she was too smart to think it was nothing more than a visit between friends. The three men had stayed ensconced in the study for quite some time after Anna and she had left, even longer after Cicely had left them. Whatever could they have had to discuss? Something else was going on. Anna was not the only one in the house who wanted to be a part of the happenings, especially when there was such a large chance it involved her in some way, shape or form.

Colleen had known by Sebastian's action that he had every intention of distracting her, but she would not be deterred. Something was going on with Cicely and Colleen was determined to find out.

Sebastian's head lifted from reading some papers and the instant he saw her, he smiled.

"To what do I owe this pleasure to, as if I didn't know."

She walked around his desk and when he pushed his chair back, she settled in his lap. It was, after all, her favorite chair in the house.

"Tell me."

He didn't even pretend that he did not know what she was asking about. With a resigned sigh, he leaned back in his chair.

"I told your cousin not to tell you and here I am about to spill the gossip. If I do, you must swear to not let her know you know."

"I swear."

He pursed his lips, then kissed her collarbone. "This is big."

"I swear. Now tell me, Sebastian."

"First, let me say that it is under control. Second, no one can know. It quite upset Cicely, as you saw yourself."

She nodded.

"It seems that Cummings accosted Cicely last night."

She gasped. "She did not say a word."

"Well, Douglas made it there before anything happened, thank God, but after a few heated exchanges, one of which Cummings apparently gloated about the fact he compromised her, Douglas challenged him to a duel."

"He cannot fight a duel."

Sebastian chuckled. "Your cousin is very capable of fighting a duel, sweetheart. But I don't think that will be tested. In Cummings' case, I have a feeling he will tuck tail and run away. The reason I tell you is threefold." He took her delicate hand in his. "One, I know you would drive me batty until I told you. Two, I think that you should be prepared in case Cicely ever feels the need to talk to another woman about what she experienced. She still seemed a bit shook up when we spoke. And three, I think that you were right about our cousins."

A grin lit her beautiful face. "I told you I saw something in the way he looked at her."

"Well, that something is a bit more than it was last night. I could feel the spark between them."

Pleased, she slipped her hands up to his shoulders and behind his neck. Both Cicely and Douglas deserved happiness. She hoped they found it.

"Are you busy at the moment?" she asked.

His hand flexed on her thigh. "Actually, I just finished working on some investments. I was thinking of taking a break."

"Ahhh, and I am at loose ends now that Cicely has left for the lending library and your mother and Anna are out for a ride with Dewhurst. Oh, and I locked the door."

As he brushed his mouth against hers, he chuckled. "How could a man want more from his countess?"

CB80

Cicely studied the weak selections on the history shelf and sighed. All that seemed to be left were historical romances. While she loved romances, she needed a good book detailing the Reign of Terror in England. There had been several intriguing clues, certain parties, people the writer knew, that might help Cicely start piecing together who the author of the diary was. If it was actually a true accounting and not fiction. Lately, as she read, her skin crawled. She felt as if she were being watched. She'd glance up furtively even though she knew Sebastian's house was exceedingly safe.

It was the book. It had that power. It sucked her in. She felt its danger, its promise. There were times she found herself lost in novels, wanting to escape into a world of the author's imagination. But this was different. Knowing there was a chance it was genuine, it was as if she were flung back into the time of the Terror. Cicely had even entertained the notion that the diary was written by a spy. In her hands was a living, breathing piece of history. How many counts of murder and intrigue had she already read through? If the men behaved even close to how they were described in the pages of the diary, she had every reason to catch her breath. They were treacherous men who protected themselves and their cause by any means necessary.

"So nice to see you, Lady Cicely," Lord Oglithorpe intoned from behind her.

She suppressed a groan and turned to face him. "Oglithorpe, how are you today?"

"Couldn't be better. Beautiful weather and now a beautiful woman." He looked over her shoulder then focused his attention on her again. "I see you, too, have come looking for history books."

It took every effort not to yell at the older man. She had been a member of The Historical Society since the age of nineteen. And here he acted surprised by her interest in the subject. She drew in a deep breath. Perhaps it was not censure or surprise. Perhaps the older man was pleased to see her browsing through the tomes.

"I was looking for a good book on England during the Time of Terror."

He smiled knowingly. "Ah, yes, your little diary."

His patronizing tone made her grit her teeth. This time she did not try to hide her irritation. "Yes, my diary. Thus far, it has been a fascinating read. It has sparked my interest in the time period. At the society," she said pointedly, "we spend so much time on the classics."

"I was wondering if you had shown it to anyone else. Sometimes that is just what a small piece of work needs. Mayhap you require an expert to look at it."

She chewed the inside of her bottom lip. "No, I have not."

"Possibly I could look at it. Give you my opinion."

She blinked at him, amazed at his interest. "But your expertise lies with the Roman Empire. While, yes, many of the same military or strategic plot devices seem to have been shared and employed in the subject's methodology, I don't see how that could help."

"All roads lead to Rome." He chuckled. "I find myself with some free time, and I thought I would offer some assistance."

His avid interest sent a chill down her spine. Other than to tell her she was wrong about every assumption she voiced during debates, Oglithorpe rarely paid attention to her. Until the last meeting. He paid her breasts more interest than he had ever given any of her discussions on history. Perhaps that was what caught his eye.

"I do not have it with me."

"I could—"

"Lady Cicely, so pleasant to see you," Dewhurst said.

When she saw the young earl standing close by, a concerned expression on his face, Cicely's muscles relaxed and relief rushed through her.

"Dewhurst?" Oglithorpe asked. "Just what the devil are you doing here?"

Dewhurst smiled. "Why, looking for some reading material. I would assume the same as you."

Oglithorpe mumbled something she did not quite hear and then said, "I will see you next week at the meeting, Lady Cicely. Remember my offer."

Rudely ignoring Dewhurst, the older lord hobbled off toward the entrance. She watched him go, wondering just what the man was about. He had never shown interest in her prior to the diary. Even then, the first time she'd mentioned it, he had promptly dismissed her. Excitement skittered over her skin. Maybe there was something to it. A man with Oglithorpe's connections in government would know if there had been a plot against the Crown. That is, if the Crown itself knew.

"Lady Cicely?"

She shook herself from her fantastical thoughts and refocused on Dewhurst. The young lord studied her with concern.

"I am sorry, Dewhurst. I was woolgathering." Then she remembered he had a date to drive about the park with Anna. "I did not expect to see you here."

He grinned and she was again struck by his looks and good humor. If only she could love a man who was so amiable.

"I just returned from my ride with Lady Anna and her mother and decided to stop by for a book or two."

"And I am ever so grateful that you did. Otherwise, Oglithorpe would never have left me alone."

"He did not overset you, did he?"

She chuckled. "Oh, no. Oglithorpe is not a problem. More of a bother, really. The only thing I worry about is being smothered by his pompous personality. Did you enjoy your ride with my cousin?"

Heat crept into his face. Oh, splendid. It seemed that to some degree Dewhurst returned Anna's feelings. Since Anna had never shown a particular interest in any gentleman, Cicely was glad that Anna's regard was returned by Dewhurst.

"The weather was superb and the company even more so. I had thought you would join us, but Anna said you were attending your own schedule this day. She did say you'd mentioned the lending library."

"Yes, I was looking for some information on the latter part of last century, but alas, there is not a good book to be found. Not that I am lacking in reading material," she said, glancing at the book in her hand. "I need to be off since we are going to be attending the theater tonight. I daresay I will see you there?"

He nodded. "I would be honored to escort you home."

"Oh, no thank you. I have a footman waiting for me, and the Ware carriage. I suppose I should dawdle no longer, as it is. Thank you for rescuing me from that painfully dull discourse."

After bidding the young earl goodbye, she checked out her book and headed through the front door. When she stepped onto the street, she searched for John, the footman who was to be waiting for her and was puzzled when she did not see him. She noticed the Ware carriage parked down the street so she turned in that direction, thinking John must have misunderstood her directions.

As she walked along, her thoughts drifted back to Oglithorpe and his odd behavior. The man never showed interest in last century historical study. In fact, she had heard him on more than one occasion say that nothing of importance could be studied until all those involved were dead. So why had he given so much attention to the diary? Could he somehow be connected?

A hand wrapped around her elbow, the fingers digging into her skin even through the fabric of her clothes. Before she could turn, she felt the prick of a knife in her side.

"Do not say a word, me lady, or I will split your gullet."

He need not fear. The same bewildering detachment she had felt when cornered by Cummings rushed over her, effectively cutting off her ability to run, to scream, to move.

Chapter Twelve

In which Dewhurst plays the hero.

Cold fingers of fear slid down Cicely's spine as she nodded to her captor. He pulled her off the street and into a nearby alley. As she desperately tried to devise some way to break free of his hold, her gaze took in the activity on the street seeking to find one person to help. This particular corner was deserted, the two closest shops no longer open. Why had she not accepted Dewhurst's offer of escort?

The stench of rotted food filled her nostrils. Bile rose in her throat as her fear doubled. Her mind whirled as she tried to come up with something—anything—to free herself of the hold of the ruffian. He was stronger than she'd gathered upon first impression. Regardless of strength, she reminded herself, the knife he held to her side cared little for station, size or shape. It could cut them all the same. She shuddered, tripping over her own feet.

"Stop your antics. I'm warnin' ya."

When he had them far enough away from the street so no one could hear her scream, or if they did, they would not think to look, he released her, pushing her roughly against the brick wall. She stumbled, but caught herself before her face connected with the unyielding brick. Even through her gloves, she felt the scrape.

When she turned to face him, her first full assessing glance at her captor stunned her. The young man could not be more than fifteen, if that. Not that it calmed her fears in the least. She knew that desperation could make anyone deadly. She had firsthand experience. The lad's hair was dark and overly long, brushing over the frayed collar of his thin coat. The cold, determined look in his black eyes sent an icy wave of horror over her soul. This was a young man who had seen the worst in life and survived, but at what cost? And at what cost was he willing to continue?

That gave her an idea. Perhaps she could plead with his more entrepreneurial spirit.

He wet his cracked lips. "I need the book."

For a second, she did not react. The comment was not what she expected. Already terrified, it took her a few seconds to work through what he had asked.

"The book?"

He glanced down at her arms, and she followed his gaze. She was holding the book she had checked out from the library against her breasts as if that could save her.

He gestured with the knife. "Come on, lady. I need—"

"Lady Cicely!"

She turned, relief replacing the terror when she saw Dewhurst running down the alley. The ruffian used the momentary distraction to grab the book from her arms and run deeper into the alley.

Dewhurst reached her. If she could just make her mind stop spinning she would be fine. It was then she noticed that John was with Dewhurst, a gash on his forehead, blood oozing from the wound. She slumped backward. The young earl grabbed her by her upper arms to steady her.

It helped, slightly, but she still could not stand.

With a sigh, she slid all the way to the filthy street. She must have surprised Dewhurst with the action, because he let go of her. The cold ground seeped through her gowns, but she didn't care how cold her bum grew or how nasty the ground was. At least she would not topple face first into the mess. Blackness pushed at the edge of her vision.

Dewhurst bent down, peering into her face. "Lady Cicely, are you all right?"

Unable to speak, she nodded.

"I am ever so sorry, my lady. One minute I was waiting for you, the next I was waking up in an alley several blocks away," John said.

She looked over at the injured footman and finally found her voice. "Oh, John, we should get you home. Someone needs to stitch that up."

He touched the wound and flinched.

"The important question is, are you okay?" Dewhurst posed the query and she turned her attention back to him. It was a mistake. The movement was too fast. She planted her hands on the ground on either side of her hips. She took three deep breaths and felt markedly more in control. Her racing heart had slowed to a fast canter.

"I am perfectly fine, except for having a bit of a fright. I just need a moment to compose myself, then we can go."

Crouched in front of her, Dewhurst asked, "What did he want?"

"The book. He took my book."

"Your book?"

The bewilderment in his voice brought a small smile to Cicely's lips. "Yes, such a silly thing, really. I have no idea why he would want a book from the lending library enough to threaten a woman with a dagger."

"Just what the bloody hell is going on here? Dewhurst? Unhand Lady Cicely."

Douglas' deep baritone sounded down the crowded alley as he strode toward them. Giddy, warm relief filled her at the sight of him. Dewhurst, apparently taking Douglas at his word, released her.

She blinked repeatedly. She should try to stand.

Dewhurst and John jerked to attention, greeting Douglas with awe and respect. Cicely fought the bubble of hysterical laughter threatening to break free. Her nerves were raw from the strange turn of events over the day and even though she felt comfort that Douglas had appeared, she could not seem to calm her heart.

When he reached her, anger darkened his eyes, and his expression was unemotional, cold. He scowled first at John, then Dewhurst. Finally he turned his stormy gaze to her, along with his steely presence and unwavering attention.

"Please forgive me for the oversight, Your Grace, but I do not believe I shall be able to curtsy."

The muscles in his cheek flexed as if he were grinding his teeth.

Her fragile will buckled, her world spun, her heart beat loudly in her ears for two, maybe three beats and then Lady Cicely sank into darkness.

CR&O

Douglas' heart was still lodged firmly in his throat as he stepped through the front door of the Ware household. Cicely, in his arms because he had been unable to let her go, had come to once in the carriage, but had since been out cold. His breath labored and speaking nearly impossible, Douglas walked through the foyer. Fitzgerald gaped first at Cicely, then at him.

"Your Grace?" The aged butler's voice was barely above a whisper.

Swallowing the panic that felt as if it would consume him, Douglas said, "Please summon Penwyth and Lady Victoria."

"Immediately, Your Grace."

But when Fitzgerald turned to leave, Penwyth was already striding down the stairs.

"Good God, Ethingham, what are you doing?"

"I am holding your cousin, who"—his voice had risen, so he modulated it—"I am to understand, was accosted over a book she checked out from the lending library this afternoon."

The earl's frown was fierce as he reached the bottom of the stairs. "What the bloody hell are you talking about?"

"I am sure that Ethingham would like to get Lady Cicely settled."

Penwyth started at the sound of Dewhurt's voice, apparently not noticing the younger man had followed behind them. When Douglas glanced over his shoulder, he found Dewhurst helping John through the door. Dewhurst fairly staggered under the young footman's weight as he guided him across the floor. The handkerchief Douglas had given him was now soaked in blood, and John had gotten lightheaded in the carriage.

"Fitzgerald, send a footman around for Dr. Thomas," Sebastian ordered.

Nodding, the butler left without a word, his face drained of all color.

"Ethingham, let's get her into the study. Lay her down on the couch. John, have Simon"—he nodded to the footman who had just walked up—"help you to your room. We will send the doctor to you when he arrives."

"What about Lady Cicely?" John asked.

Douglas could tell the words cost the lad much. He paled further at the volume of his voice.

"She needs the doctor first," John said.

Douglas inclined his head. "We'll see to her safety. You take care of yourself."

Sebastian ushered Douglas into the study where he efficiently swiped the sofa clean of pillows. When he stepped back and gestured it was ready, Douglas could not seem to bring himself to put her down. Tucked safely in his embrace, she felt so small, so fragile and defenseless. God help him, but he would never forget the bone-chilling fear he felt when he discovered her in that alley. Dewhurst standing over her, fading footsteps of the assailant sounding in the distance and young John bewildered and bleeding. When he'd found out she had left the lending library five minutes prior and never made it to her carriage, panic had held him by the short hairs. Five minutes… Anything could have happened.

Douglas pulled her tighter to his chest. His arms trembled, but it was not from her slight slip of a form, it was from her danger and his shortcomings. The fact that it had been Dewhurst and not himself who had saved her had struck him to his core. It was asinine and juvenile, but he felt he had the right to be the one to protect her. But he had been too involved in other things, too busy to keep up with her comings and goings.

He looked down at her. Her color was pale although her breathing was deep and steady. She was so cold. So lifeless. So unlike Cicely.

Penwyth stepped forward and said in a lowered voice, "It is all right, old chap. The doctor is coming. She is safe. She is going to be all right. Just set her on the sofa and we will figure it all out."

Before he could embarrass himself by refusing to set her down, she stirred. Her heavily lashed lids fluttered, once, twice, then rose. The instant fear that leapt in her eyes twisted his heart. But that fear dissolved into confusion when she realized who was holding her.

"Douglas?"

Penwyth coughed discreetly behind Douglas, apparently taking note of Cicely's familiar use of his name.

Without paying attention to the other man, he placed her on the sofa, knowing now that she would be fine. She blinked up at him as he straightened. He knew the moment she remembered the incident. What little color was left drained from her face.

"John?"

Of course. Her first concern would be for someone else.

"He's fine. A doctor is going to have to stitch up the gash, but he will be hale and hearty soon enough."

She nodded then turned her attention to Dewhurst who had just stepped through the door to the study. "Thank you so much, my lord. If you had not come upon us when you did, I shudder to think what would have happened. He was a desperate lad."

Her thin voice sent another wave of rage pouring through Douglas. He did not like the mind-numbing fear, the desperate worry that the incident had caused him. The sound of her weak voice had him lashing out at Dewhurst.

"Yes, just how was it that you should be the one to discover Lady Cicely was in trouble?" His tone reeked of suspicion but damned if he could stop it. The giant green beast that was jealousy clawed at his belly, fighting to get out.

"Chance only. I saw John wandering down the street covered with blood and I had just talked to Lady Cicely in the lending library. She had said John was to escort her home so when I found John, I realized something terrible had happened. We started our search immediately, and I am thankful she had not been taken too far."

Douglas opened his mouth to ask what had prompted them to turn down that unlikely alleyway when Colleen rushed into the room, followed closely by Lady Victoria and Lady Anna.

"We just heard what happened," Colleen said. She was composed but he recognized the same fear in her eyes when their gazes met. Her attention turned to Cicely. "Cicely." She hastened to the sofa. "How are you doing?"

Cicely smiled weakly and looked a bit embarrassed by all the attention. "I am fine. All the excitement and skipping luncheon probably caused my fainting spell."

Douglas thought it probably had a bit more to do with nerves, but he remained silent.

Anna, looking much like a woman warrior, settled her hands on her hips and faced Dewhurst. "Just what is this all about?"

Douglas smiled with humor and compassion. It was about time that someone asked that. Perhaps the domineering little woman could coax answers he himself could not.

"Anna, please. He saved me from a ruffian who apparently was after my lending library book."

161

Suddenly Anna's demeanor changed. Anna cast a worshipful glance at Dewhurst and then turned to Cicely. "A book from the lending library? How utterly absurd. Why would a man of the streets be interested in that?"

"I have no idea, truly. It is not as if it was worth much and I was carrying more valuable things in my reticule than that book."

Sebastian stirred at that comment. "What exactly did the man say?"

Cicely slowly turned her head. "He said he needed the book."

"Odd, that." This came from Dewhurst.

"What was the book about?" Douglas inquired.

Cicely struggled to sit up. When Douglas opened his mouth to tell her to settle down, she shook her head. "Do not worry, Your Grace. I just need to sit up and think."

After she settled she said, "It was a biography of George Washington."

"What the bloody hell would he want with that?" Sebastian asked.

"Sebastian, tame your tongue," Lady Victoria said.

Cicely blinked, then rubbed her eyes. The pain, the remorse and the worry shone brightly in her gaze. "It is a bit overwhelming that a man would attack John and threaten me over a book about the first president of the colonies."

Silence greeted her statement until Anna spoke up. "I bet it has to do with that foolish diary you've been reading."

"Oh, Anna," her mother sighed. "You are letting your imagination run away with you."

"What diary is that?" Douglas asked.

"Really, Anna—"

Anna drowned out Cicely's denial. "She has that diary that tells of a plot to overthrow the Crown, or it seems that is what it is."

Another beat of silence filled the room. In the next instant, it exploded in a rash of questions, everyone trying to talk over the others.

"Silence!" Sebastian yelled. They all turned to the earl, who now stood behind his desk. After affording them a look of censure, he fixed his attention on Cicely. "Cicely, what is this about?"

Cicely smiled weakly. "The diary I bought. It looked like a diary about society here in England during Napoleon's reign. And on first look, I am sure most people would assume, as I did, that it was no more than a particular gentleman's views of parties and whatnot. But then it changed. There was more detail about a group he was involved with who thought the Crown had too much power."

"And you think that is when they started plotting to overthrow the King?" Douglas asked.

She sighed. "They had started out simply enough. They wanted more rights for the common man, and rightly so. But there was a change along the way. It became more about their destiny, what they felt was their right and duty to overthrow the Crown."

"Treason," Dewhurst said.

"At the very least," Sebastian concluded. "There might have been other crimes they committed along the way. Who knows what is in that book, what it might uncover."

Cicely shook her head. "I have yet to determine its authenticity and who the people involved were."

"You have yet to discover?" Douglas asked. "You have been researching it?"

She nodded. "There has not been much interest in it before now, as many of the members of The Historical Society scoffed when I approached them with my discovery. Well, until Oglithorpe started taking particular interest in it."

"When was that?" both Sebastian and Douglas inquired.

"Well, I know he asked me about it several times in the last few days. Then, this morning, he cornered me at the lending library. That was right before Lord Dewhurst happened along to save me from being bored to death by the offending man. His area of expertise is in the Greco-Roman Empire. As a matter of fact, he has oftentimes spoken out against researching or listening too keenly to recorded recent history. He says that until all of the parties involved are dead, no one can ever truly uncover the details of what happened."

Bubbling with excitement, Anna said, "I think—"

"Anna, why don't you and Dewhurst take some tea with Mother? I am sure that he is famished after his afternoon of adventures."

The abrupt order caused Anna to frown at her brother. "But—"

"Lady Anna, I would be pleased to take some tea. I daresay Fitzgerald could rummage up a few of those biscuits I like so much."

Anna looked to argue, her lips compressing into a thin line, but one more glance at her brother and she relented. Once Dewhurst and Anna, along with Lady Victoria, were ushered out of the room, Colleen shut the door behind them and nodded to Penwyth.

"Why did you send Dewhurst away?" Cicely asked.

"Anna would have never left on her own." He frowned. "And no matter how much I am in his debt for his rescue this afternoon, he is not family. And the less people who know about this, and everything in it, the better."

Colleen nodded. "I agree. We keep this within the confines of the family. Let's sit and discuss the matter."

After they had all settled, Cicely told them of the plot, summarizing as best as she could, of the five men of Quality and their plans to help Napoleon's revolution spread to England.

"But, I am only three-fourths of the way through the diary and the code names make it impossible to decipher who they actually are. There is some detail about the scandals of the day, society information, but not really that much to go on."

"And that is why you went to the library today?" Penwyth asked.

"Yes. I was hoping to find some historical books on the time period so I could match what is in the diary to the events. Maybe even another diary of someone in the Realm. Perhaps it would show me a pattern and link some of the names to the code."

Penwyth looked at Douglas. "Have you seen this?"

"No. But I think it might be about time to have a look at it."

გზეი

"I heard there was an incident this afternoon," Jupiter stated.

Noir's heir grimaced. "Yes, someone accosted Lady Cicely and from all accounts, stole her book."

Jupiter turned his attention from the younger man and looked out over the square located across the street from his house. Afternoon traffic was light, mostly last-minute calls and those heading home to ready for dinner or an evening filled with balls. It had been years since he had worried about exposure. Years in which he had carefully built a fortune that would dissolve under the scrutiny of treason.

"Do you think they made the connection?" he asked, knowing the answer, hoping it wasn't true.

"Yes."

Sighing, he faced the younger man who still had the look of his father. Many people saw those affable looks, the pleasant smile, and misjudged the creature that lay beneath. Out of all of them, Jupiter knew Noir's heir was the most calculating. He followed in his father's footsteps. It had been Noir's plan and the others had accepted it and the opportunity and all that came with it. They all enjoyed their little society. They had done terrible things, but Noir had always been much colder, sadistic. If rumors proved true, the son was even worse.

"It is a problem," Noir's heir said.

He nodded. "Yes, it is. Especially since the gossipmongers are all atwitter about the thief asking about a book. Then stealing it from her, at knifepoint." A chill settled in his blood. "That is not a good thing. People get interested, more will speculate."

"And there seems to be a connection between Lady Cicely and the Duke of Ethingham."

"Damnit. Do you think he is after the diary?"

Noir's heir shook his head. "I have a feeling he's after Lady Cicely."

Jupiter grunted and they descended into silence, both men contemplating the implications of that. The younger man broke the stillness.

"I wanted to offer my condolences on the passing of Raven."

"Why? The man was as useless today as he was all those years ago. He and his errant ways were one of the reasons we had to dissolve. Other than Napoleon's defeat that is. Bastard could not keep his mouth shut around his mistresses." He settled in his favorite armchair, his bones aching with age, with regret. "Do you think you can take care of Lady Cicely?"

The younger man nodded. A smile curled his lips. "I will make sure it is taken care of as soon as possible."

Chapter Thirteen

In which Lady Cicely finds more pleasure than
expected at the theater.

"We should not have come tonight."

Annoyed, Cicely listened as Sebastian stated his feelings on the subject for the fourth time since they had arrived at the theater. She had long since abandoned any thoughts of changing his mind. Arguing would not work, and they had already arrived. The point was moot.

Colleen sighed as she stepped around Lady Randel. "Sebastian, if you say that we should not be here one more time, I will throttle you. And if I cannot finish the job, I am sure either Cicely or Anna would gladly help." Her tone softened. "Cicely said she's fine, and I, for one, believe her."

Sebastian opened his mouth to argue, ignoring the looks they were drawing. He was stopped by Bridgerton's arrival.

"Say, old man. Lady Cicely, Lady Anna and of course Lady Colleen. Dewhurst."

His voice dipped when he said the other man's name and Cicely noted the barely veiled look of hatred he hurtled in Dewhurst's direction. The apparent vehemence was masked before Cicely could make heads or tails of it, although she did remember his obvious irritation with Dewhurst before tonight.

She glanced over at Lady Anna, who looked to be trying her hardest not to sneak glances at Bridgerton.

The talk descended into inane comments about the upcoming performance and she allowed her mind to wander. The day had started out with a burst of excitement, and with everything that had happened, Cicely felt a bit weary. Still, she was glad to be out of the house. After the attack, she had retired to her room to read over the diary. She spent the entire afternoon steeped in conspiracy and threats to the Crown and was in dire need of a break.

There was a stir within the crowd. She turned to where many of them had fixed their attention and saw Douglas striding toward them. He had that confident, loose-limbed kind of walk that spoke of his place in society. It was as if he were a great leopard winding his way through a pack of hyenas. The moment she met his gaze, her heart turned over. Never had she had a man look at her with such a predatory air, as if he would fight to the death to gain her attention. Even though she was sure she was imagining it, Cicely could not stop the little thrill of excitement that danced through her.

Ignoring society's rules, he threaded his way through the milling crowd, barely acknowledging acquaintances. He never once took his attention from her face.

Considering their last talk together, she had not been sure how he would act tonight. Douglas had behaved as boorish as her cousin. Since she was already overwrought, she should consider her health.

As Douglas neared, anticipation mounted, from her and everyone who witnessed his behavior. In her mind, she knew his devoted interest was not proper. But with her body humming and excitement skating through her blood, it was hard to do anything but return his regard.

By the time he reached their group, murmurs had risen in speculation, but for once, she ignored them.

"Your Grace," she said, dipping into a curtsy and bending her head. As she rose, she met his gaze, allowing her lips to curve. She was rewarded with a flare of heat in his eyes.

He bent over her hand, kissing just above the skin, as was proper. Even through the thin material of her gloves, she could feel his breath against her flesh and shivered in reaction.

"Running late tonight, Ethingham?" asked Sebastian. There was a devilish gleam to his eye that, when Douglas looked at him, he returned.

"Just had a few matters to attend to."

After Douglas made that cryptic statement, Sebastian nodded ever so slightly. No one else seemed to notice. The crowd started slowly moving toward their boxes.

Douglas offered her his arm. "I would be honored if you would allow me to escort you to my box."

"Your box?" she asked, even as she rested her hand on his forearm. Was he proposing they be alone in the box? It would be highly improper of him, but it was such a delicious idea.

"I told Penwyth my box would make more sense. There is more room for all of us."

She stifled a sigh of disappointment. She knew it was not appropriate for them to be alone, and Douglas would never damage her reputation. Still, it would have been exciting to start her lessons tonight. Anna demanded her attention with a comment about Colleen's dress and Cicely pretended to listen. She nodded and laughed, offering polite rejoinders.

"You're flushed. Are you sure you are well?" Anna whispered.

"Yes, I'm fine." She waved her fan in front of her face. "It's rather warm in here."

"That it is," Anna replied and plunged off into another diatribe about how exciting it was to be sitting in the duke's box.

Cicely nodded, but she was agreeing for another reason. The thought of being near Douglas, and for the first time ever knowing her presence affected him, was exciting to say the least. Her skin tingled, her breasts ached.

As they all entered the box, she brushed by him. Every muscle in his body seemed to freeze as the heat between them rose. He let loose an audible breath. She glanced in his direction and watched him visibly swallow. The brief contact had her head spinning, but at least she was sure now that he was suffering as much as she. Once they were settled in their chairs, with Douglas to her right, she put her plan into action.

Douglas shifted uncomfortably in the heavily padded chair, trying to ease the ache in his loins. There was no way around it. The chit was driving him mad with lust and she was doing it on purpose.

At first, he had not been so sure. For the first ten minutes, he surmised it was possible he was simply going insane. If the daring emerald dress she wore, one that dipped too low in the bodice in his opinion, was not enough to drive him crazy, he did not know what would. Yet not too far along in the first act, she had started enticing him. Nothing openly solicitous, nothing that any sane person would question. But he had moved past that point long ago. She would touch her hand to her earlobe, a simple gesture. In his mind, he could think of nothing but how it would feel to pull the delicate skin between his lips and suck. That had been bad enough.

Then the glances began.

Nothing untoward, but enough to catch her eyeing him as if he were a particularly forbidden treat she wanted to sink her teeth into. Practiced courtesans could take lessons from this virgin, who until recently had never had a breath of scandalous behavior attached to her name. She knew just what to do to tease, drawing in a breath so deep her breasts threatened to spill out over the bodice of her dress.

Another rush of blood drained from his already addled mind, heading straight for his groin. If this kept up, by the time intermission arrived he would not be able to walk upright. He certainly could not stand and make polite conversation.

Just then, she glanced at him, then to those who surrounded them, and lifted her gloved hand to the neckline of her dress. Touching her index finger to the satin material of her neckline, she slipped her finger down the edge, following the top line of her bodice.

His cock twitched. He followed the movement with his gaze, aching to be the one to touch her. She sighed, and he found it hard to suck in a breath. Unfortunately for him, she did not. Another deep breath and her flesh rose above the neckline. He licked his lips, imagining running his mouth over that skin, plunging his tongue between her breasts—

Applause rang out. His fantasy dissolved into a puddle of frustration. He raised his gaze to meet Cicely's and found her watching him out of the corner of her eye, her face still forward.

Irritation intermingled with his arousal. The impossible woman knew exactly what she was doing. Lord help him. He had yet to truly begin their lessons but she already understood how to tease. What would she be like twenty years from now?

That thought reminded him of his own plan. Apparently their time together had intrigued her. She wanted another taste of passion, and Douglas was willing to accommodate—to a point.

C820

Cicely wandered down the hall to where many of the men had disappeared to smoke their cheroots and discuss matters they deemed important. She sighed at her snippy thoughts, but she could not help it. Her body was a mass of nerves, throbbing with arousal. She had planned to drive Douglas to distraction, which she was pretty sure she had accomplished. The only problem with that was what it had done to her.

She now found her body sensitive to everything. Every time the fabric of her dress moved against her breasts, her nipples hardened. Cicely was mortified that while teasing Douglas during the first act, she had grown damp between her legs.

A door opened and as luck would have it the object of her thoughts stepped into the hall. He did not see her at first. But the second he did, his body stilled.

"Lady Cicely."

She smiled and walked forward. The closer she drew to him, the more worried his expression grew.

"Douglas, if I did not know better, I would think you are avoiding me."

He glanced first one way and then the other down the hallway. Grabbing her by the arm, he hurried her to a door, which he opened. Not releasing his vise grip on her arm, he poked his head in the room. He must have decided it safe, for after a moment he pulled her through and slammed the door shut behind them.

"Just what the bloody hell are you doing?" His tone was low and angry.

Cicely hesitated. What if she had read him wrong? What if he no longer wanted to continue with their liaison? But beneath the anger, she heard the frustration. She recognized the same feeling he brought about in her.

"I wanted to talk to you."

She did her best to pout, but she had never been that good at it, and the room they were in had little to no light.

"I think talk might be a dubious description at best, Cicely."

She chuckled. "There is that."

He stilled, his body seemingly focused on her. "You wanted your first lesson tonight?"

Was the man thickheaded? "Of course."

Even now, the delicious thrill of being alone with him had her body responding. Her muscles tensed, her breathing grew fractured. He was close, so close she could detect the faint scent of his cologne. With it mostly dark in the small room, her other senses heightened. Douglas shifted his weight, his body barely making a sound, but she heard it. Knew the discomfort she had caused, and for the life of her, she could not feel guilty.

What she felt was exhilarated. Her skin prickled with excitement as heat rushed through her.

"I had thought you would allow me to pick the time and place. The Throckmortons' house party later this week would be better. What am I thinking? Of course, you would not wait for me. You are the same woman who propositioned me on a dance floor."

The thread of warm amusement, not to mention the deepening of his voice, told her that he approved of her actions. She moved closer, her skirts brushing his legs.

"I would wait for you forever, Douglas, but right at this moment it would drive me insane."

He snorted. "And just what would you wait for?"

She said nothing as she slid a hand up his arm. If he truly knew her feelings, that she had decided days ago he was the only man who could be her teacher, he would refuse her. It was only the threat of her going to someone else that had him acquiescing to her demand.

"We do not have time for much, I know. But I thought maybe something..."

She allowed the implied question to hang, the implication being that she would take what he was willing to give. As close as she was now, she could make out some of the features of his face. The flash of white against the darkness took her by surprise.

"Something?" His voice dipped into seduction. "I think that I might just be able to accommodate you, my lady."

He bent his head and brushed his mouth over hers. Slowly, surely, just enough to entice, to whet her appetite. His tongue flicked over her lips. She gasped, half in excitement, half in invitation, but he moved away before taking the kiss further.

"One of the things you need to learn, my dear, is taking the time to enjoy."

She opened her mouth to blast him, but it came out as a moan when he cupped his hand on the underside of her breast. Damp heat surged through her as he moved his thumb over her nipple. Back and forth, barely touching her, he continued while he slipped his hand around her waist, pulling her closer.

"Patience is a virtue, Cicely." Her breasts swelled, her mind blanked. "One that can bring about the best of rewards."

He tugged on her bodice. The delicate fabric gave way easily, her breasts springing free. Cool air slipped over her heated flesh. Douglas bent his head and when he spoke next, his breath warmed her nipple.

"And sometimes, that reward is best shared."

When the tip of his tongue touched her nipple, she gasped again. Once, twice, he moved his mouth over her, laving the turgid peak. As he continued, he shifted his hand to her other breast and caressed the sensitive underside.

"So sweet," he murmured against her skin.

In the next moment, he took her nipple into his mouth. Her lungs seized, then released the breath with a moan of his name. Allowing her head to dip back, she closed her eyes, enjoying the wicked feel of his mouth on her. Under their own accord, her hands raised to the back of his head. She speared her fingers through his hair, reveling in the thick, rich texture before molding her hands to the back of his head.

The heat that had gathered in her belly twisted and warmed then slid between her legs. She needed more. She needed his skin against hers, to be able to touch, feel, tease, just as he was doing.

But before she could voice her desire, he jerked away from her. She opened her eyes as she stumbled back against the wall. The only sound in the room was the faint singing from onstage and their heavy breathing.

"I believe that is enough for lesson one."

He was not serious, was he?

"We need to get back before anyone notices our absence."

He was!

The scoundrel. Her heart still beat a tattoo against her breast, her body still buzzed with arousal, and he was stopping? Was he not affected the way she was? Did his body not need a release, to lose himself in her as she wanted to drown in him?

"Douglas—"

"For the love of Christ, woman, could you pull up your bodice?"

The shakiness of his voice caught her attention. He was still breathing heavily and he had turned away slightly. She had thought him controlled, but she'd been wrong. Even though she was still disappointed that he stopped, she did as he asked.

"I think you need to return by yourself." He looked at her. "And allow me to pick the next time and place. This was inventive, but it does not have the amenities one needs for a liaison."

Miffed that he did not appreciate her tactics, and still more than a little aroused, she said, "Of course, Your Grace."

He chuckled but did not move to touch her. Instead he opened the door, and after checking the hall, stood back to let her slip through. As she made her way back to his box, she tried her best to get her body under control, but it was hard. Harder than she expected. What little had happened in that room had her ready to rip off her clothes and offer herself up to him. Just what would he have in store for her next?

Chapter Fourteen

In which the duke is offered advice.

Cicely looked over a particularly interesting passage, frowning over the strange comments from the diarist. There was a listing of their names again, those other four he had conspired with, but right after that he mentioned how he and Digby had made contact with the French government, then run by Napoleon. The intricacies of their plan made her head pound, but if she understood it correctly, they'd offered to house French assassins.

Excitement raced along her skin. Could Digby be one of the five? It seemed quite possible. She wrote down the name, linked it to Scarlet, the writer of the diary.

"You look like you found something?" Lady Victoria's voice made Cicely jump. "Oh, I am sorry, dear. I did not realize that you did not hear me enter."

She turned and smiled at her aunt. Dressed today in her favorite violet, her delicate beauty was easy to discern. "Do not worry. I just found a name mentioned here. It is before your time, but do you know the name Digby?"

Victoria pursed her lips in thought. "Digby. Hmm, there was a younger son, one with a horrid reputation." She *hmm'd* again, then her eyes widened. "Of course! The Earl of Sheffield."

"Sheffield? Why does that sound familiar? I do not think I know any of them."

"Oh, lud no. The only one left was Digby, his real name was...Diggory." She made a face. "There is a good reason why he went by Digby, I daresay. Why did you want to know?"

"His name is mentioned in here."

Victoria's eyes widened. "Well, that would be understandable. That family was never good ton. They had been at one time, but they had a run of bad luck, bad earls and a few scandals. Digby finally got the earldom a few years ago when the last earl dropped dead in a brothel."

"Why would that name be familiar to me?"

"He just died. There was not one male heir left, so the earldom is basically dead. He owed money all over town from what I understand."

Cicely sighed. "Another dead end."

"Oh, no." Victoria slipped onto the settee next to Cicely. "What we need to do is pick my memory to figure out who he was friends with at the time."

"This was before your time, and I think that afterward, they would have done little together."

"He had been good friends with a baron...but there had been some kind of scandal." She was quiet for a few moments and Cicely tried her best not to be disappointed. Although it was a good find, without a living heir there was not much to go on.

"Chambers!"

Cicely jumped again. "What?"

"Baron Chambers. They had been friends at one time, and then... I am not sure, before my time as you say, but something happened between them."

"Were either of them married?"

"No. Which is odd because both of them were the end of their line."

Another false lead. "Well, maybe there is something there. I will definitely check all of that out, but I am not sure where to get more information on old scandals."

Victoria chuckled and patted Cicely's hand. "I am meeting today for tea with old Lady Smythe. She knows everything in society. Even at her age, she has a mind as sharp as a knife."

After a discussion of possible leads and who Victoria should approach, she left, and Cicely sank into her thoughts, the mystery of the diary fading now that she had to wait for answers from her aunt. It had been three days since her first lesson. She had seen Douglas since, but they had always been surrounded, once in the park and twice here at the Ware household. They had not yet had a chance to steal away to move onto their next lesson.

Tonight was the last night before they all left for the Throckmorton house party. She knew from past experiences it would be relatively easy to grab a bit of privacy, but it was hard being patient.

And he knew it would be. That is why he did what he did, promised her gifts for her patience. He was trying to heighten her experience. While she appreciated his thoughtfulness, it was truly driving her mad.

She sighed, running her hand over the diary. Cicely knew pushing him would not work, but she worried. From his past behavior, his interest in her would wane soon. She had accepted that, accepted that she would end up being hurt in the end. But she would rather have one taste of passion with Douglas than spend the rest of her life wondering what she had missed.

Knowing there was nothing she could do, she decided to get back to work on the diary and try her best to put Douglas out of her mind for now.

ᏟᏰᎬᎠ

Douglas frowned at the cravat his valet had fashioned for him.

"Are you sure this is not too intricate, Robinson?"

The older gentleman's eyebrows rose, not in question, but irritation. "I believe that you should trust my opinion and knowledge, Your Grace."

"I *believe* you would have me dressed like a popinjay if I gave you a chance."

Robinson harrumphed. "Is your current state of irritability due to the fact we will have a new duchess soon?"

Damn the man. For all the years he had been with Douglas, Robinson never missed anything. By the time he had his first pony, Robinson had been in charge of Douglas' life. From his short pants to his first year in society, Douglas had counted on Robinson. Even during the darkest of days, Robinson had tried to protect Douglas, and nurse his wounds when he could not. Even so, there were some things a man liked to keep to himself.

"And why would you suspect that?"

Robinson held up a coat, shaking it, silently ordering Douglas to come to him. Douglas sighed and did his valet's bidding. What good was a title when he was ordered about by servants?

As he helped Douglas on with his jacket, Robinson said, "You have not been out late, except for those nights you are out with your cousin's family. I assumed your interest lay with one of her new family."

Douglas said nothing, irritated that he was that transparent.

"It is not as if it is that hard to figure out, Your Grace." He brushed Douglas' shoulders. "And if I may be so bold—"

"Oh, please."

"I believe it is time you found someone to marry." He stepped around Douglas and started tidying up the remnants of his preparations for the ball that night.

"You believe I should marry. How nice that you want me to be doomed to matrimony." Douglas tried to inject humor but even he knew it fell flat. "Worried about the lineage of the dukedom?"

Robinson stopped his work and faced Douglas. Time had thinned the man's auburn hair. The laugh lines around his mouth and eyes had deepened with age, but added character. Douglas now topped him by almost half a foot, and looked down instead of up at him.

"You mistake my reasoning, Your Grace."

"Never mind, I was only jesting."

Robinson's gaze turned speculative. "You think I do not know why you never entertained the idea of marriage?"

Uncomfortable with the frankness of the question, Douglas shifted his feet. It was as if the last twenty years had not happened.

"You think you have tainted blood. I know, I see by your expression I am right."

He flexed his hands, thinking they were larger than his father's had been. "You know what first-class bastards both my father and grandfather were. Would you not wonder the same thing?"

Robinson sighed. "Aye, I would. I had a bastard of a father too." That bit of information took Douglas by surprise. "Did you not wonder how I knew your worst fears, where you would hide?"

Douglas shook his head.

"I lived through the same terror and ran away at the age of ten and three. I barely survived, but the day your grandmother walked into the inn where I cleaned slop and hired me is a day I will be thankful for until I die."

Douglas felt a lump rise in his throat as he watched the man's eyes fill. He had always thought of Robinson as an older brother. He had been the one who taught him to ride, how to smoke a cheroot and helped him recover from his first night of drinking to excess.

Robinson cleared his throat. "Now, you will be late, and I doubt you would want that, Your Grace."

Douglas nodded, but stopped when he placed his hand on the doorhandle. He turned and said, "Thank you, Robinson."

"Just make sure you return with that cravat in decent shape."

"Robinson."

The valet looked up from his work.

"Thank you, for everything."

He nodded and went back to work, although Douglas was sure he heard the man sniff.

By the time Douglas made it to the Endintons' ball, it was in full force. The crush of people had risen to an uncomfortable level, the heat of the ballroom overwhelming.

He spotted Cicely almost immediately. The ton's apparent fixation with Lady Cicely had yet to wane. Every eligible bachelor, even some of those who had sworn no interest in marriage, gathered around her vying for attention. When Douglas came upon the scene, he ground his teeth and pushed his way through the crowd. He stopped short when he found Bridgerton standing to her left. The impassive look he gave Douglas irritated him even more. Douglas was sure now that the earl knew of his intentions toward Cicely. If Bridgerton thought he could make a play for her, he was sadly mistaken.

Cicely, who had been engaged in talking to Scotty Farrington, the younger son of the earl who was hosting the ball, noticed him. Her eyes widened, then warmed. A smile curved her lips.

She offered her hand, which he took, and curtsied. "Your Grace."

He waited for her to rise, then bent over her hand and murmured, "Lady Cicely."

After releasing her hand, he felt the pause in the conversation around them. Every eye was watching them, weighing his behavior and that of Cicely's. Irritated that he had to do this in front of an audience, he shifted to her right, taking his place next to her. The look he gave the other gentlemen was met with a mixture of expressions ranging from irritation to fear to outright anger. Even so, the conversation continued. Cicely had maneuvered the discussion back to the diary. Now he understood why Bridgerton was standing guard.

"Lady Cicely." Lord Oglithorpe—who was for once not talking to her breasts—said, "Have you had any experts look over this diary?"

He felt Cicely stiffen. The cut to her research skills and intelligence was so obvious, the murmurs around them rose.

Douglas, outraged on Cicely's behalf, opened his mouth to put the old man in his place, but Cicely did not allow him the time.

"Since I am not sure if it is real or not, my lord, I see no reason to worry on that. My own research ability is fine enough for a project like this."

She turned away, trying to dismiss the man, but he would not let the subject go. "But, forgive me for saying, you are a woman and therefore unable to discern the possible intricacies of historical review."

"Really?" The tone of her voice, not to mention the way she drew out the word, signaled to Douglas that Oglithorpe was in trouble. The smile she offered the older gentleman had nothing to do with humor.

Oblivious to the rise in animosity not only from Cicely, but from some of the other women in the crowd, the old goat continued on, digging a much deeper hole. One Douglas was sure Cicely would gladly bury him in. "Of course, at your young age, you would not understand that a woman's mind cannot work through every detail. Females are known to be flighty, and therefore cannot focus on serious historical study."

By the time the ass finished, Douglas could feel annoyance vibrating from Cicely. A flush of anger crept up her neck and into her face. She leaned forward, ready to strike out at the windbag. Douglas glanced over her head and noticed that Bridgerton's shoulders were shaking in silent laughter. Douglas would get no help from that corner.

Cicely would take a lot of things. She would take people attacking her looks, her ability to hold polite conversation, even her prospects of marriage. But she would not take any slight to her intelligence. Soon, her temper would take control and Lord only knew what would happen then.

"Lord Oglithorpe—"

The sweep of bows across strings interrupted Cicely's attack. Understanding he needed to save her from an embarrassing scene she would later regret, he lightly touched her elbow to get her attention.

She started and turned to look at him. The irritation still darkened her eyes, and the wonderful flush left her skin all rosy, as if she had just risen from bedding a lover.

Moving away from that thought, for now at least, he said, "I believe I have this dance, my lady."

Her eyes narrowed slightly, but she said nothing. Just nodded and after excusing herself from the crowd, allowed him to guide her to the floor.

Once there, she came into his arms without hesitation. He knew no one could tell by her actions, or her expression, that she was irritated. She was the picture of a serene lady of Quality. But in the last few weeks, he had come to know her expressions well. And this one boded ill for Oglithorpe if she did not get over her anger.

Her eyebrows drew together in a frown, the skin between them crinkling. Her posture was stiff, formal, as was the smile she afforded him.

"I know you are angry with me."

Her gaze moved to his, then slid away again. She said nothing as he turned them around the floor. Inwardly, he chuckled. This woman actually thought she would not make a good duchess. She had the imperious look down pat. She would rule his home with no problem.

"I wanted to save you from making a spectacle of yourself."

Again, she looked at him. "Truly?" The incredulous tone in her voice, not to mention the snort that followed, told him he had not convinced her.

"Punching a man in the middle of a crowded ballroom—no matter how much he deserved it—would only draw more attention to you. And not the type you would want."

She harrumphed. "I daresay it would have been worth it."

"Nevertheless, it would not allow us our next lesson."

That bit of information caught her unaware. But she recovered nicely, even if she spoke with a bit more breathlessness than before.

"Your Grace, I cannot wait to see what you have to teach me tonight."

Just that little breathy sentence and the deepening of her voice had his body reacting. His blood heated and his cock throbbed. Being this close, holding her thusly was driving him mad. The dip in her voice signaled her arousal, but she did not know what she had been missing. He did, and he intended to show her tonight.

"As I said before, patience is readily rewarded."

She looked up at him through her lashes, the act so overtly coy but innocent at the same time, it struck him in the gut. What he was doing, seducing a young woman because he needed her, was not the most honorable thing. But Douglas could see no other way. If he declared himself immediately, she would panic and run from him. If that happened, he was truly not sure what he would do.

As the waltz drew to a close, he maneuvered the dance, ensuring they ended up near the French doors that led to the patio. With the supper hour drawing near, he hoped that many of the people would be inside looking for partners. His theory proved true as they stepped out and found the area deserted.

"Where are we going?"

He looked at her and his heart dropped to the pit of his stomach. In the moonlight, her skin shone as if it were fine porcelain. The violet dress she wore clung to every curve, accentuating that tiny waist and full bosom. But it was the look of excitement in her gaze that struck him to the core.

"I know of a room with a lock."

She giggled. "Lead on, Your Grace."

Taking her hand in his, he did just that.

The room that Douglas had in mind was indeed perfect for seduction, thought Cicely. A branch of candles cast dancing shadows along the walls, and a fire had been lit. The coziness of the room made her think that their hosts had left it to welcome liaisons.

The click of the door lock caused Cicely's heart to jump a bit. She was not sure what Douglas had in mind for tonight, but a strange mixture of apprehension and anticipation wound through her.

She did not turn around as Douglas moved toward her. He stepped up behind her, sliding his arms around her waist and drawing her against him. His body heat warmed her but she shivered. Not because she was cold but because he was doing absolutely delicious things with his lips to her neck.

He chuckled, his breath feathering over her skin. "Like that?"

She nodded, then bent her head to the side to allow him more access. His lips moved over her, nipping and licking. His teeth grazed the sensitive flesh just behind her earlobe.

"What did you have in mind tonight, Douglas?"

He paused and slowly turned her around. "I think it is better if I surprise you."

Pulling her close, he took her mouth in a kiss that spoke of not only passion, but possession. She twined her arms behind his head as his hands slipped around her waist and pressed her against his aroused body. When she felt his hands on her bottom, she gasped, and he used the opportunity to invade and conquer. His tongue tangled with hers, a dance of seduction on another level.

Just as the night at the theater, her body reacted on some primitive level she did not fully comprehend. Her flesh grew damp and her nipples hardened—begging to be caressed. As if he heard her thoughts, he moved from her mouth to her throat, nipping and kissing until he reached her neckline. Baring her breasts, he skimmed his mouth over them, arousing one, then the other. With each touch of his tongue to her flesh she lost another bit of her grip on reality.

In the next moment, her world turned on its axis as Douglas lifted her and placed her on the desk. Before she could understand what was happening, he was pulling away from her, getting down onto his knees in front of her.

"Douglas?"

He smiled. "Trust me, love."

She pulled her lower lip between her teeth and nodded. Without taking his gaze from hers, he grabbed hold of the skirt and slowly eased it up her legs. His palms followed the silk, skimming along her thighs. Her heart was now beating out of control, her face burning with embarrassment. But she refused to look away. Instead, she held his gaze boldly. At that, his smile widened, warmed. Mesmerized by it, and the corresponding heat in his eyes, she did not realize at first he was sliding her legs apart and slipping in between them. Before she could react, he bent his head and pressed a kiss on her inner thigh.

Heat shot to molten lava within her veins. She opened her mouth to reject this action, to tell him it was not right. What she had wanted to say dissolved the moment his tongue skimmed the skin just above her stocking. Her senses thrilled, her nerve endings danced. The scrape of teeth, the swipe of his tongue, he continued his actions as he moved up her leg. Closing her eyes, she ignored the rising physical discomfort that had her wanting to stop this insanity. But somewhere, somehow, she knew it would cause more pain to stop.

He carried on with his assault until he reached the apex of her thighs. Alarm shot through her as she felt his breath on the most private part of her body. Her eyes flew open, her mouth followed to reprimand him. She was wet there, her body melting under his masterful assault, but when she gathered her wits and tried to close her legs, he ignored her. She expected him to comfort her, tell her not to worry, but he seemed transfixed. Without a word, he pressed his mouth against her.

"Douglas!"

He did not even flinch at her shout. Instead, he applied himself to licking, touching and kissing her intimately. Her breasts ached, her body throbbed. Cicely knew she should stop him. What he was doing was not right, could not be right. But the warmth of his mouth had her softening to his demands. He positioned his hands beneath her bottom and pulled her closer, feasting on her as if she were his last meal.

Not able to speak, not willing to ruin the delicious decadence he worked on her, she closed her eyes again. His fingers dug into her rear end as he persisted. His siege against her senses toppled every defense she had against him. Her body tightened, wet heat surged. Fire blazed a path along her flesh.

The muscles that had tensed now grew almost unbearably tighter. She shook her head, trying to grab control of her sanity, but he continued. His mouth grew more insistent as he worked, and her body responded. Nerves grew taut and she felt like she was racing toward a goal she did not know or understand. And still, he continued. His hands were moving over the globes of her rear end, her skin putty beneath his palms. Smoothly, easily, he pushed her, prodded her to the finish. Understanding that he would catch her, that he knew just what she needed, she surrendered—her body, her soul—to the pleasure that called to her. Heaviness gathered between her legs as he held her closer. His tongue flicked over some pressure point and the dam broke. She moaned his name as she shattered into a thousand pieces, her body convulsing.

Weak from her release, she bent forward. Douglas rose to his feet, drawing her tight against his chest. Her ear rested against him and she could hear his heart pounding almost in tandem with hers. Lifting her head, she looked up at him. The heat in his eyes still lingered and she realized she had received her relief, but he had not.

"Douglas—"

He stopped her with a kiss. The musky taste of her passion filled her senses, the knowledge of that both wicked and thrilling.

They were both breathing heavily when he pulled away. He rested his forehead against hers. "Do not worry."

"But, you did not..."

His smile was gentle, loving. It did more to her composure than the seductive ones he had bequeathed on her earlier.

"No, but this was not for me. This was for you."

Knowing now, even as she tried to gather her wits, what it meant for him to go unfulfilled moved her. The sacrifice, not to mention the gift he had given her, touched her heart, warmed her to her toes. She understood it represented more to her than it did to him, but still she had to tell him her feelings. She needed to convey everything it meant to her, would mean to her in her memories.

But the only thing she could do was lean her head against his chest and say, "Thank you."

Chapter Fifteen

In which Lady Cicely takes the initiative—as all women should.

Douglas walked wearily to his bedchamber, trying to keep his thoughts straight and his irritation beneath the surface. Since they had arrived at the Throckmorton house party, Cicely had been driving him mad. What was he saying? She had been driving him mad from the moment she asked him for lessons.

She was not overtly flirting with him. But, through the course of the trip here, and the time they had spent together, she had done her best to entice him. Just like at the theater, her glances were above the detection of most others. But with each look, each brush of her body against his, she pushed him further.

Since their last lesson, he had spent most of his time half aroused. It had been a painful few days and her behavior had made it worse.

He reached his door and opened it, stepping over the threshold with a sigh. He was tired, but sleep would be hard to come by. He had not had a decent night's sleep in days thanks to denying himself pleasure. But it was not the right time, the right place. Initiating Cicely before he received her acceptance of marriage would be foolhardy. And would disrupt his plans.

Oh, but it would have felt so good to sink into her, feel her muscles tense around his cock. He closed his eyes as his blood drained to his loins, and his body, already hard, grew harder. He wanted to lose himself in her, forget memories of his past that had been bothering him as of late, and just enjoy. She would accept him for who she thought he was. And knowing that was killing him little by little.

He groaned, his frustration growing.

"Is there something wrong, Douglas?"

He heard Cicely's voice but did not open his eyes. Instead, he wanted to wallow in the idea, the fantasy that she was here with him. He heard movement on his bed and he willed his eyes to open.

There, sitting in the middle of his bed looking like a treat waiting to be enjoyed, sat the object of his thoughts, the star of every one of his fantasies.

Irritated, already aroused, he said with too much force, "What the bloody hell are you doing here?"

Instead of scaring her, or even deterring her, she smiled. "I've come for my next lesson."

"You what?" His voice had risen and he sounded like an offended spinster.

Again, she paid no notice as she slipped from the bed and walked toward him.

She wore nothing but a sheer nightgown, white in color and almost transparent thanks to the fire glowing behind her. She approached him on bare feet, her steps barely making a sound as she crossed the floor. She stopped less than a foot away.

"I said I have come for my next lesson."

"But—"

She chuckled and moved closer. "But nothing. You promised more when we came here and it has been two full days. I cannot wait much longer, Douglas."

Excitement dripped from her voice and scattered his good sense.

"You cannot?"

She nodded and placed her hands on his chest. "Since our last time together, there has been a...need growing. A need for you."

He shook his head, trying to gather his wits, trying to gain some sense of control, but failing.

A frown turned her mouth down as she stepped away. The space gave him the chance to take a breath, but that only brought in the scent of lavender and aroused woman.

"I do not want to wait and I demand more." Her tone dripped with authority, but he did not miss the catch in her voice. Because of that, he did not expect her next move. He anticipated retreat. Instead, she bent at the waist, grabbed the end of her nightgown and pulled it with a jerk over her head. Tossing it behind her, she stood in front of him, hands on her hips, her chin lifted proudly.

He had never seen her completely nude, but there she was, gloriously naked. The fire blazing behind her lent a warm glow to her porcelain skin. As his gaze traveled down her body, he paused at her breasts. He had seen them, but not thusly, completely free of clothing. Full, bottom heavy, with the most delicious pink nipples... He licked his lips. He slid his gaze on down her body, delighting in the fact that she never moved. When he looked back up at her face, he noticed a blush had covered it. It added to the delectable package that was Cicely Ware.

Something warm shifted through him to his heart. It spread throughout his body, causing his stomach to tighten and a lump to rise in his throat. He cleared it and attempted one last time to play the hero.

"I do not want to take advantage of you."

For a second she said not a word. And that was all it would take. One word and he would do anything she wanted. One command and he was hers. But then she laughed and shook her head.

"Douglas, what more do I need to say? I would not have followed you to your room had I not trusted you implicitly." Her gaze did not waver. Her expression did not change. "I want you to take advantage of me, Douglas. In fact, I believe I told you that almost a fortnight ago. I asked you to. Since I asked, does that not mean it is no longer 'taking advantage'?"

From the moment she asked him for lessons on that crowded dance floor, she had been leading him around with little to no problem. She had slithered beneath his skin, curling into his heart. Teasing, tempting, calling to him, asking him to take that which he did not deserve. He had decided years ago not to marry, not wanting to pass on his poisonous genes to another generation of innocents. But as she stood there, nothing but firelight covering her skin, he felt his steeled control slipping.

"I remember." His voice was hoarse with need. "I wanted to ensure you had no regrets."

Cicely searched his face. He felt himself leaning closer, losing himself in the depths of her wide chocolate brown eyes. In them he found comfort. He found friendship and a kindred spirit he'd not expected to ever discover. She soothed him much like a sweetened confection. Douglas attempted to move away from the nearly overwhelming temptation. Before he could,

Cicely grabbed his hand. She held on with a death grip and rubbed her thumbs over the sensitive skin on the back of his hand. Her brow wrinkled as she watched the motion. Douglas swallowed. Her heat warmed him as she touched him, her fingers still moving over his flesh.

"How could I regret the one thing I know would make me complete?" she asked.

Slowly, she lifted his hand to her mouth. As she did, her gaze rose to meet his. They locked with each other in a battle of wills. She deliberately turned his hand over and kissed the palm, flicking her tongue against him.

Another surge of heat ran along his nerve endings and settled heavily in his loins. She kept him trapped there, not allowing his gaze to leave hers, keeping his hand against her mouth as she said, "I want you to make me feel. I want you to make me forget."

He was back to shaking his head, trying to hold onto the last vestiges of his honor, when she moved his hand from her mouth and placed it on her breast. She killed him with one word.

"Please."

In that single request, he heard a need that matched his own. He was damned tired of keeping himself apart, of being aloof. He wanted to forget the world and fall into her. All he wanted to do was be there, as one with her.

With a groan, he yielded. He gently pushed her backward to the bed, tumbling them both onto it. He kissed her, but this time he held nothing back. Douglas wanted her to know him. He wanted her to understand that he needed her more than his next breath of air. His words were lacking. This he was good at. He'd held back before, trying not to scare her, but now there was no reason to. She returned his kiss with a yearning he could feel all the way to his soul. Her response increased his own desire, brought forth his darker passions. Breaking from the kiss, he placed a trail of wet kisses down her flesh, delighting in the taste of her, the feel of her skin beneath his mouth.

When he reached her puckered nipple, he paused, licking his lips in anticipation. How this woman hid the wonder of her figure from society, from him, for so long, he had no idea.

She drew in a deep breath, her sweet flesh quivering with the action. He bent his head and flicked his tongue over the tip. Her breath came rushing right back out. He smiled and took the entire nipple into his mouth. With his hand, he stroked her other one, bringing it to a tight rosebud like the first. Her moans grew, the sound of them pounding through his blood, encouraging him, emboldening him.

Knowing that he had to have more, that he had to make this first experience perfect, he moved away from her breasts. Even in the darkened room, she could not hide the aroused flush that darkened them to the tips of her nipples. He slid down her belly, delighting in the flesh as it quivered, in the salty-sweet taste. When he reached her core, he breathed in her scent. Aroused woman surrounded him, stirring his passion even more. Her uneven breathing hitched as he gathered her up for his taste. She tensed briefly but then relaxed against the bed.

As before, when his tongue stole inside for a taste, the flavor of her essence filled his senses, spurred his arousal. Never before had a woman tasted as if she had been created just for his pleasure. He could hear his name on her lips, the passion in her moan. His body grew taut, blood surging to his cock, twisting his balls. Soon, her legs moved restlessly against the bed and she threaded her fingers through his hair, fisting, pulling, urging him closer. Grabbing what little control he had, he slipped one finger into her, preparing her for his entry.

Christ she was tight.

Driven by his own desires, he flicked his tongue over her hardened nub. She shouted his name, her body first tensing, bowing off the mattress before she convulsed. He lifted his head, replacing his tongue with his thumb and watched in fascination as her mouth opened in a soundless cry.

He knew if he did not have her at that moment he would go completely insane. Surging up to his knees, he yanked his trousers open. His shaft sprang free, a drop of moisture already wetting the head. When he looked at Cicely, she eyed him with wonder instead of the maidenly fear he expected. He had to push her hand away when she reached out to touch him. Without a doubt, at this point he would embarrass himself if she so much as breathed on him. He would be lucky to last three thrusts.

"Not...right...now," he ground out. Urging her back, he covered her body with his and slowly eased into her warmth. He closed his eyes as her muscles clamped around his cock. Lord Almighty.

As he pushed further in, he felt the barrier of her virginity and paused. "Love."

Her eyes fluttered open.

"This will hurt."

She nodded and closed her eyes. He drew back slightly and surged ahead, breaking her maidenhead. Possessiveness roared through him, touching something deep within him he had not known he possessed. It was primitive and overwhelming, but the fact that he had been her first almost pushed him over the edge.

"I'm sorry, love, it couldn't be helped." He couldn't believe how wonderful it felt, her heat, her core, her embrace. He struggled for control, waiting for her.

Without opening her eyes, she said, "It isn't so bad."

He snorted at her faint praise. "I promise it will get better."

Without another word, he dropped his head to her shoulder, resting his forehead against the sweet curve of her neck. Pulling back out and then thrusting back in, he could not stop the surge of joy that shot through him as he built his pace. Her body grew damp and pliant beneath him. Still, he had to grit his teeth as he fought against the escalating need for release. He wanted to prolong the pleasure for as long as possible. Not only for her, but for himself. He shut himself off from everything except her and what he was feeling, tasting, smelling. Soon Cicely joined in, catching his rhythm and moving with him.

He slipped a hand between them and flicked his finger over her hardened nub again. Her second orgasm caused her to scream his name, which he tried to swallow by capturing her mouth in a kiss. Her muscles tightened, then quivered around him, pulling his own release from him.

Moments later, he collapsed on top of her, his body, his mind, his soul sated. She hummed, the sound filled with satisfaction. As if she were a kitten with a bowl of fresh cream.

He lifted his head and looked down at her. Her lips were reddened from his kisses, her eyes heavy lidded from spent passion. As he eased away, he stripped out of the remainder of his clothes and joined her beneath the covers. Part of him was well pleased with what had transpired. The other part of him was shaken to the core. Never had he lost complete control of the situation, given to a woman a part of himself he knew could be twisted, used and then tossed away. But he had.

He waited for fear or panic to grip him but there was nothing. Only peace filled him as he lay back down beside her, drawing her close. She snuggled closer, her body relaxing against his, her hand over his heart.

"I believe that went well, Your Grace." She giggled, apparently pleased with her formality when they were both nude. He responded with a smile. He'd noticed these past weeks she had been laughing more frequently, and the careless sound slipped right under his defenses and captured him. "I have to say, I now understand what all the fuss is about."

He chuckled. "And that was just one experience."

He felt her raise her head and he opened one eye to look at her.

"There's more?" He did not miss the excitement in her tone, or the flush that was now darkening her skin.

He groaned. "I have created a monster." With one hand, he grabbed her by the back of the neck and brought her down for an openmouthed kiss. His body stirred, but he knew they both needed a break. Him for rest, her to recover. After he finished kissing her, he shoved her against his chest.

"Get some rest, then we'll see."

"But—"

"Go to sleep, Cicely."

He closed his eyes waiting for her to argue, but she gave up her quest, softening against him. Moments later, her breathing deep and even, he relaxed, his own mind drifting into nothingness.

CRSO

Cicely moved her hands over Douglas' bare back, tracing the faint scars that marred his flesh. They were not that easy to see in the dim light of the fire, but she could tell they had been brutal.

"Where did you get these?"

He tensed and the moment of silence stretched.

"Tell me."

For a moment, she was certain he would not. He rolled to his side and propped his head up with his hand. The pain she saw in his eyes, the nightmares she could almost feel, held her still. Waiting. Silently she pled with him to share, to give to her some bit of him. She worried he would not, especially when he laid on his back and stared up at the canopy on the bed. But as if unable to hold back, the story poured out.

"I spent most of my childhood at the estate, like many children of station. My parents kept me out of the city, telling people they did not want their son to be exposed to the unhealthy air. They would explain how I was a distraction and my overabundant energy would drive them batty within a day. But, they truthfully kept me in the country to hide the bruises."

She bit her lip to keep from gasping.

"You see, the Dukes of Ethingham have a penchant for making money and beating the bloody hell out of their children. Father believed in beating the devil out of an ill-mannered child, me. But he had nothing on his father. My grandfather was a world-class bastard. I know why my aunt ran, not only for love, but to escape."

"Oh, Douglas." She blinked back the tears, her heart breaking for the boy who had suffered.

He didn't seem to notice her words. He sank further into his memories, despair etched over his proud face, and continued, completely wrapped up in the retelling. "There was
202

nowhere to hide when he was in a bad mood. Even in that cold estate with its multitude of rooms, if he was mad at you, he would find you. It could last for hours, days. It took me years to realize that the sadistic old bastard enjoyed the hunt. My parents would leave me for weeks on end with a man who hated me."

She slipped her hand up to cup his face. "I am so sorry."

"I do not want your pity." His voice had turned harsh.

Cicely started. "I am not offering that. Maybe I have some for the little boy who was betrayed by people who should have been protecting him. But the man I know, the one I love, is not that frightened boy anymore."

He huffed a breath, then swallowed. "That is why I stayed off the mart so long. I swore I would never submit a woman or a child to that. I worried since both my father and grandfather were abusive that their blood tainted me in some way."

"Despite the horrible childhood you were forced to endure, you have become a man people admire, and I know deep within my soul, that you would never hurt another human being for pleasure, especially not a child."

He studied her face, his gaze moving over her features. "You're sure of that?"

She did not hesitate. "Yes."

With a groan packed full of surrender, he grasped her hand and used it to pull her closer. She fell over him, her breasts flattened against his chest. He took her mouth in a kiss that had her body humming within moments. It possessed. It declared ownership. Something she would give now, forever.

He rolled her over, stretching his body on top of hers, and said, "I do believe it is time for lesson two of the evening."

CR&O

Douglas watched Cicely tie the ribbon at her throat, then slide her feet into the slippers. Brushing a hand over her hair, she smiled at him.

"I guess I should be getting back."

The sun was not even peeking over the horizon, but Douglas agreed she needed to go. Soon, the house would start to buzz with the early-morning work of servants. But he did not like it. He wanted her in bed with him.

He rose and felt a spurt of pride when her gaze roved down his nude body in appreciation. Pulling her into his arms, he gave her a quick, hard kiss. "We have one more night here, but then once we get back to London, we can start planning."

"Planning?"

"Our wedding."

"Wedding?" She blinked and just like that her expression shuttered closed.

He pulled back slightly. With horror, he realized they had not discussed the implications of their actions the night before. A small coil of unease whipped to and fro in the pit of his belly. Her tone. The deceptive calm, the careful silence following her words, made the unease shift rapidly to panic. "Is something amiss?"

She pulled completely out of his arms and cleared her throat. "Nothing except there is no reason for us to marry."

He bit his tongue. Their entire relationship had been too rash. He grabbed a pair of pants and stepped into them. After he fastened the last button through its hole, he said, "Other than the fact I just took your virginity?"

"Do not be silly. You took nothing. I gave."

He opened his mouth to argue his point, but she stepped forward and brushed her mouth over his.

"Have you married every woman you have been with?"

Heat filled his face. "No, but that was different."

She shook her head. "Douglas, really, marriage was not part of the bargain. I did not ask it of you before. I do not ask it of you now."

"What if I say it is?"

She moved away, frowning. "I beg of you, do not make this more complicated than it already is."

The panic clawing his gut had him rushing forward. He caught her before she unlocked the door. She looked up at him, questions in her gaze.

"I plan on making it more complicated, more than you can imagine."

She grimaced. "Douglas, I do not want to argue with you, and I have to get back now."

Knowing she was right, he acquiesced. He unlocked his door, checking the hallway for people. Finding it clear, he slid back inside. As she moved to leave, he stopped her by placing a hand on her arm.

"Just know that this is not the end of this conversation."

She searched his gaze with her own then nodded before slipping out into the hall. Closing the door behind her, he sighed. He should have known she would not agree to marriage, or be coerced. It would take more than losing her virginity for Lady Cicely Ware to accept marriage. What that one thing was, he had no idea, but he would find out.

And she would find just how hard it was to tangle with a duke.

Chapter Sixteen

In which a villain suffers a mishap.

Cicely stared out at the pouring rain, her melancholy almost suffocating her. It had been a week since they had returned from the country, and she had yet to get Douglas alone. He still gave her those heated looks and danced every waltz with her. Citing her loss of virginity—which she told him did not bother her in the least—he claimed they must marry. Each day she could tell he was chomping at the bit to go to Sebastian and confess everything that had happened.

She sighed, thinking once again that she had not chosen wisely. Oh, she could not have picked a better partner, the man she loved—even if he was being a complete drudge about the whole thing. He had shown her such tenderness, such love that she knew that she had been right.

But she never counted on Douglas getting morals. Seriously, if a man was a rake, he should not change his colors. Why was it that men just could not seem to stay the same?

"Cicely?" Colleen called from the hallway.

"In here."

Colleen stepped into the room and smiled although worry tinged her gaze. "Sebastian wants to go over some things Daniel found out about your diary. Do you have it with you?"

She shook her head. "No, it is up in my room."

"I will send Fitzgerald to get it."

"Oh, no. Let me. I need to freshen up."

Colleen smiled. "We are in the study so just come back down when you have it."

When she reached her room, she found the door slightly ajar. Cicely was of a habit of closing her door because the draft sometimes caused the door to slam. Thinking one of the maids must have left it open on accident, she pushed it open further and then closed it behind her before she saw the figure by the window.

"I've been waiting for your arrival, Lady Cicely." Cummings' voice was hoarse, and he bore no resemblance to the man whom she had seen weeks before. He was wild, dangerous and desperate. He had not shaved or, from the stench, bathed. The hair that had never been out of place now stuck out in all different directions and his clothes looked as if he had rolled about in rubbish.

The only thing that looked new and in working order was the pistol he leveled at her.

"I would advise you not to say a word, my lady, or it could end badly for you."

"If you think that I will go with you, as if Sebastian would give you money if you forced me to marry you, you have gone completely mad."

He laughed, the sound of it so cold it sent an icy chill filling her heart. "I do not give a bloody damn about marrying you. Hell, I cannot even imagine being shackled to you and that load of bothersome family."

"Then what do you want?" She tried to keep her voice steady but she knew he had heard the catch.

"The diary."

That made her pause, her mind going completely blank. "The diary?"

He snorted. "Of course. I need it."

"You want to research my diary?"

"No, you stupid bitch! My father was one of the five."

Every preconceived notion she had before she walked into the room shattered. "Your father plotted treason?"

His face turned purple with rage. "Yes, the miserable old bastard. It is just like him to leave me a damned mess to clean up. Where is it?"

She nodded toward her bedside table and he motioned with his gun for her to retrieve it. Her breathing had grown shallow, her pulse beating an erratic rhythm.

"So who was your father?"

"Does it really matter?" When she just turned to look at him, he grunted. "My father was Noir."

She hoped Cummings did not notice how slowly she was walking. "And so, you found out by..."

His eyes narrowed. "You are walking too slow. It took me days to break in here, and I will be damned if you are going to screw up my plans. Get the damned diary."

Cicely opened the drawer, then reached in to lift it out.

"It's all there? You've not pulled out any letters?"

"That's it."

"Now, over to the window."

She paused and he chuckled. "You did not think I could just leave, did you?" He tsked. "I cannot go on with my life if you are here. And surprisingly, I can say with all honesty I'm sorry. I never wanted to hurt you. I tried for it not to come to this."

"Why did you risk it? Letting me find out who you were?"

"I had no choice. Every day was a day closer to you discovering who they were, who we were. It would ruin all of us, but especially me." He motioned with the gun. "Now, come along. The craziness that had plagued your mother has now taken you over, you see."

"No one will believe that."

He cocked his head to one side and smiled. "They will. Since you returned from the country you have been out of sorts, everyone has mentioned it."

The horror of the situation caused her to follow instructions. She could not think, could not even devise a plan when she was sure she would die. When she opened the window, cold rain pelted her dress and her face. Drawing back, she turned to face him.

"Step up, my lady."

"No." If she was going to die, she was not going to make it easy on him.

"I will shoot you if you don't."

It was her turn to smile evilly. "Go ahead. A shot would bring everyone running."

His mouth tightened slightly and he looked out the window behind her. Then, he rushed her. She was ready for it and although she had nowhere to go, she braced herself for the blow. Both of them stumbled back against the sill. Rain dampened their clothing as they struggled over the gun. Cicely knew she needed to get the gun away from him and only then would she have a chance to run. So with every bit of her energy left, she wrapped her hand over his wrist and dug her nails into his skin. He cursed, his finger flexed and the gun went off. The bullet pierced the glass, shards of it falling on the two of them. She kicked him in the shin, and he dropped to the floor, taking her with him. He landed on top, pushing her against the broken glass.

As they struggled, she heard the door open.

"My lady?"

Betsy. "Run, get Sebastian!"

Cicely felt a short spurt of relief when she heard Betsy's footsteps retreating. Cummings immediately sprang up and tried to reach for her. Cicely scooped up the diary and attempted to get away. He grabbed her by the ankle, his fingers digging into her flesh. With what little strength she had, she kicked at him. His fingers slipped away as he stumbled back to the window, losing his balance. She heard the thump of footsteps approaching down the hall and watched in horror as Cummings lost his footing completely and struggled with the drapery. It was of no use. As he fell out the window, the drapes went with him.

"Cicely!" The terror in Sebastian's voice made her realize he could not see her.

"On the other side of the bed, Sebastian."

He rushed over and sighed when he found her. "You can come in, Colleen, it is all clear."

He gathered Cicely in his arms and rose to place her on the bed. Fitzgerald and a number of servants came pouring into the room.

"Send someone around to the magistrate, and get someone down there with Cummings."

Colleen sat beside Cicely and took her hand between her own. "All will be well."

The tears she had held at bay during the brief ordeal gushed out. All of the fear she had been able to ignore came rushing back and she started to shake.

"What the bloody hell is going on here?" Douglas' voice cut through the chatter of people working to clean up the mess.

She turned, her heart warming at the sight of him, but her shaking increased. He hurried to her side as Colleen, clearly reading his intent, slid off the bed. The anger and fear that contorted his handsome features caused another well of tears to overflow.

Without a word, he leaned forward and gathered her into his arms, pulling her onto his lap. She felt his lips brush her hair.

"Don't worry, love." No one said a word for several moments while Douglas rocked her. But she knew that she needed to tell them.

"He was Noir's son."

"From the diary?" Sebastian asked.

"Yes." She took the handkerchief that Douglas offered and blew her nose. "He said so when he showed up. He planned on stealing the diary and making it look as though I had gone mad."

Bridgerton came through the door, his clothes drenched, signaling he had been outside. He took one look at her on Douglas' lap and raised an eyebrow, but said nothing about it.

"What did you find?" Sebastian queried as Bridgerton accepted a towel from Colleen.

"Not much. He didn't survive the fall. I take it he was after the diary?"

She nodded and looked down at the vile piece of history with aversion.

"I wish I had never found the stupid thing." She drew in a shuddering breath. "Who cares about people who plotted against the Crown a generation ago?"

"I can assure you the Crown does, Lady Cicely," Bridgerton remarked.

Before she could ask just what he would know about it, Anna came running into the room, all the color drained from her face. "What has happened here?"

Everyone began to talk at once, their voices rising to a painful level. Cicely closed her eyes and laid her head on Douglas' shoulder. She shivered and he pulled her closer.

Sebastian took control of the situation. "I think that maybe we should allow Cicely some time to recover. Fitzgerald, get a bath brought up to the blue guestroom. Cicely will not be able to stay in this room tonight."

Douglas carried her down the hall to the blue room. After settling her on the bed, he brushed his thumb over her eyebrows. She smiled slightly, her eyes still closed. He knew she was dozing.

The blinding rage squeezing his heart, not to mention the fear that had almost unmanned him, started to fade. Love warmed him as he watched her snuggle into the pillow, wanting more than anything to join her there. It was his duty, his right to comfort her, but he knew society rules would never allow it.

"Douglas." Colleen's soft voice cut through his thoughts and brought him out of his trance. He turned and found her waiting by the door. Betsy, who had recovered from her own crying jag, stood ready to assist if need be and the message could not have been clearer. This was not his place. He was not needed.

Even though it hurt his heart, he left her and followed his cousin out the door. With one more look over his shoulder at Cicely, he vowed that before too much longer, he would not only have the right to be there with her, he would demand it.

Chapter Seventeen

In which Lady Cicely gives an ultimatum.

Two weeks after Cummings' death, Cicely thought she might very likely kill her entire family. Their gentle reassurances and tender care had been just what she needed immediately following the attack. She had been fragile at that point, and their attention had helped her through those first few days. Never in her life had she felt so loved and comforted. Even Douglas had been conscientious and gentle, but if they all did not stop she swore she would strangle each and every one of them.

"You look a little flushed, my dear," her aunt said. Cicely pointedly ignored her and watched several young debutantes giggle as Douglas walked by on his way back to her. "Cicely?"

She sighed. Her family meant well, but the need to kill them might overwhelm her better judgment.

"Aunt, please do not worry. The ballroom is a little warm, that is all. And here is Douglas with refreshment. I will be fine."

Douglas handed her a glass of champagne and studied her with concern. "I think Lady Victoria might be right. It was too much to expect you to come back into society so quickly."

She should have been happy. The attention he had shown her was everything a woman could want. Every wish she wanted had been filled, even before she thought of it. But the novelty had worn off quickly. The one thing she could not stand was being treated like she were made of glass.

"I am fine."

She noticed her aunt and Douglas share a speaking glance. Irritation had her lifting her glass of champagne and downing it in one gulp. She ignored the interest of the bystanders and handed the glass back to him. He took it, brow furrowed in worry.

She needed to get away. "If you will excuse me?"

Her aunt and Douglas again looked at each other, but said nothing as Cicely turned and walked toward the hallway that led to the retiring room. Several people tried to engage her, but she rudely snubbed them. She was sick to death of playing a role, of pretending she was someone she wasn't. Sick to death of being hovered over. She loved her family, and their behavior since the attack had been understandable. But, while she recognized their need to attend her, she could not accept it anymore. If she did, it would be accepting the fact that she was not strong, that she could not handle herself. She could and had before. This was not the most terrible thing she had been through. She had seen and weathered much worse and if one more person said she was in frail health, she would do harm to their body.

After finding the retiring room practically empty, she took a moment to compose herself. It would not do to have a screaming fit in the middle of the ballroom. People tended to notice when you went completely insane like that.

She knew they thought her in a delicate state and each and every one of them assumed it was because of the attack. While that had been decisively unpleasant, it paled in comparison to the way Douglas was now treating her. Since the altercation, he had remained by her side, but there was something missing, some distance he put between them. It was as if a stranger had taken over his body. She ached to have the man who had teased her, who had opened his heart to her about his childhood...

She was in no physical pain, but this loss was greater. Her heart was breaking. Cicely had known it would come, had known that some day he would retreat. But she had not expected it so soon, or for it to hurt so badly. His offer of marriage had been because of what they had done, not because of love. Granted, if she had said yes, he would have married her. But each day, she would have died a little. His attention would not have stayed fixed on her and he would have strayed from their marriage.

Knowing if she did not pull herself together and return to the ballroom soon someone would show up and herd her back, she shook herself free of her morose thoughts and decided to get back to the ball. She patted her hair and put her handkerchief back in her reticule. Seeing the tattered diary there, she sighed. She should not be carrying it around, but she had forgotten to leave it behind. The small book fit in the confines of her small reticule, but now she knew why it had been so heavy. Shaking her head, she closed the clasp. As she stepped out into the hallway, she stopped short, finding Douglas leaning against the opposite wall.

"What are you doing here?"

He smiled. "I was waiting to get you alone."

Her heart danced as excitement threaded through her. "Oh, really?"

"Yes." He sighed. "We need to talk about marriage again."

All her ideas and fantasies dissolved with that one demand. So cold, so unloving, so…well, not what she wanted.

"No, we do not."

He frowned. "Why are you being so stubborn about this?"

"Because, I do not want to marry." Not without love.

"It is an obligation, one we both have to each other."

Anger and pain pierced her heart and left it to bleed. "I do not want to be an obligation."

She was close to tears. They burned the backs of her eyes and clogged her throat. She refused to lose all in front of him. Brushing past him, she convinced herself she could make it back to the ballroom without further embarrassment.

Douglas would not let it go. His fingers curved around her arm and stopped her. "Cicely."

"I need the one thing you cannot or will not give. If marriage is the only option, I regret to say that our affair is at an end."

With a jerk of her arm, she pulled away. Thankful he did not pursue her, she kept walking. When she saw Lady Catherine approaching her, she blinked, trying to stave off the tears. Lady Catherine stopped by Cicely's side, concern darkening her fair features.

"Lady Cicely?"

Cicely shook her head and brushed past her. Pain sliced at her heart and she could not speak, especially with one of Douglas' former lovers. Happy when the woman decided to leave her be, she turned a corner and walked into a solid wall of a man. Looking up, she recognized the features of the boy—not to mention the smell—from the day in the alley. At first, her mind would not work, her body frozen. But she gathered her wits and opened her mouth to scream. Before the sound could escape, she felt a hard whack against her head and she sank into darkness.

CRED

Douglas' mind was still reeling from his argument with Cicely. He could not see why she was being so stubborn. A marriage between the two of them made sense.

What was it she wanted from him? He had made his intentions clear. He wanted marriage and he would not back down. The attack a couple of weeks ago had made him more resolute in his belief. She needed to be protected and he wanted to be the one who gave that to her.

It was not as if she did not know he loved her. He had showed her in every way possible. She was innocent to many of the ways of the ton, but she had to know his actions the last few weeks had not been normal—especially not for him. He had ignored any overture and waited for the one woman he wanted. The one who offered everything he wanted, but held back the one thing he needed.

Cicely could not be so thickheaded that she did not realize he loved her, could she? She was much too bright not to discern his feelings. But he thought of her expression, the trembling of her body. He'd heard the tears in her voice, the pain of her defiant position.

Cicely had no idea that she held his heart in her hands.

With that revelation, he turned back to the ballroom and ran into Catherine. The air rushed out of both of them and he had to steady her.

"Douglas."

After making sure she was okay, he released her and said, "I would like to chat but I have someone—"

"Someone took Lady Cicely."

That stopped him. "Someone? Who?"

"I have no idea. I heard something, but could not quite make it out, so I decided to return. She had been crying"—she shot him a dirty look as if she knew it was his fault—"and I wanted to check on her. She was being taken away by some man, young, with another one, dressed well enough. I yelled but there was no one around."

"Where were they going?"

"How am I supposed to know?"

They both hurried down the hall to the foyer of the house. They reached it, just as Bridgerton was walking through the front door, an expression of intent etching his features.

"Your Grace."

"Not now, Bridgerton, someone has taken Cicely." He pushed past the earl but the man stopped him.

"It's Dewhurst, and I have a lead about where he might be."

CℨℬↃ

Cicely's head pounded as she licked her dry lips. She opened one eye, then the other and looked around the room. Rising up, she realized she was sitting on a moth-eaten settee. As she glanced around the dark room, she noticed broken bits of wood, trash and more dirty furniture. Two doors, on opposite sides of the room, were closed. The stench of rotted fish filled the air. Needless to say, she did not recognize her surroundings, but her gaze fell upon one man she did. She blinked, wondering if she truly saw who she thought she did.

"Dewhurst?"

He looked over at her and smiled. "At your service."

"What? Why?"

Her brain still throbbed from the hit she had taken and she raised her hand to rub her temple. It came away sticky with blood.

"Sorry about that, Lady Cicely. I have been trying for two weeks since that idiot Cummings botched the job to get up into your room to retrieve this." He held up the diary. "But I was thwarted at every turn."

"So you decided to abduct a young lady, which in turn will bring more awareness of our situation?" The older, cultured voice was familiar and she turned her head. Lord Oglithorpe hobbled closer, shaking his head. A look of regret and pity passed over his face as he studied her.

"I could find no way to retrieve the diary. You and I both know each day she got closer to the truth." Dewhurst sounded as if he were a boy denied a reward.

"What..." She swallowed the bile rising in her throat. The fear clawed at her belly, her heart. "What is going on here? I cannot believe your only interest in the diary is for research."

Dewhurst laughed, although it was not a pleasant sound. It bounced off the bare walls of the small room, a thread of evil darkening it. "Research! No, you idiot."

"Dewhurst—"

He turned on the older man and shouted, "No, you be quiet. If it were not for your idiocy a lifetime ago, I would not have had to do this. I would be married, happily, to Lady Anna. Instead, I have lied and killed to cover up your treason."

Cicely gasped and her gaze flew to Oglithorpe. "You are one of the five."

He bowed. "Jupiter, at your service."

Her attention moved back to Dewhurst. "And you? Whose heir are you?"

"Noir."

She shook her head. "No, Cummings said he was Noir's son."

He snorted. "Well, he lied. I know, hard to believe that such a thieving, buggering idiot would, but there you have it."

"He was Noir's son, but not his heir," Oglithorpe said.

Dewhurst turned around abruptly and raised his hand. It was then she saw the small pistol he was holding. Her fear increased tenfold as her mind raced from one idea to the next on how to get out of there.

"What the bloody hell are you rambling about?" he asked the older gentleman.

"He was your half brother. Your father had an affair with Cummings' mother, ohh, just about the time your mother was pregnant with you. He was Apollo's heir"—his gaze moved back to Cicely—"but Noir's son."

"You lie! My father was ever faithful to my mother."

Oglithorpe cackled at that. "Your father was as faithful as a tomcat. He liked anything that smiled and flirted, especially if it was a pretty woman. Who knows how many bastards—"

Dewhurst pulled the trigger, the deafening sound of the report causing Cicely to cover her ears with her hands. A look of mortified surprise lit the older man's features and he stumbled back against a tattered couch, his hand clasped to his chest. Blood oozed around his hand, a violent stain against his white linen dress shirt.

"You lie." Dewhurst's voice had turned wooden, but there was a hint of madness to it. When he looked back at her, cold panic slipped over her heart, freezing her soul. The lunacy she saw shining in his eyes convinced her she would die next. She had done so many things she regretted. At the age of six and twenty, she had not yet truly lived, had not experienced half of what she wanted, and she had not told the man whom she adored that she loved him. That was the one thing she would never accept, that she did not tell Douglas of her true feelings.

He raised his weapon, aiming it at her head.

"I would rather you not shoot, old chap."

She closed her eyes at the sound of Douglas' voice. Hope shimmered through her, but she was afraid that she had dreamed him up.

She heard Dewhurst shift his feet. "What the hell are you doing here, Ethingham?"

Still afraid Douglas' voice had been a figment of her imagination, she opened her eyes. The sweet relief she'd felt was soon followed by horror. Dewhurst now had the gun pointed at Douglas.

"I have a bit of a problem." Douglas' tone was calm, as if he were discussing the weather.

"A problem?" The disbelief in Dewhurst's voice caused a bubble of hysterical laughter to rise, but Cicely fought it back.

"See, you abducted and threatened the woman I love." He shoved his hands into his pockets. "I have a small problem with that."

"Douglas."

He ignored her, as did Dewhurst.

"And I would rather you take your shot at me," Douglas said.

Dewhurst laughed, the sound now slipping into a maddening snicker, one you would expect to hear in bedlam. He raised the gun, his laughter dying into a smile filled with menace. "I aim to please, Your Grace."

Panic, fear and outright terror pushed her to her feet. Before she could reach Douglas, another movement caught her eye. A man came charging out of the darkness on the other side of the room. She could not react because someone else was tackling her, both of them falling to the floor. Her head hit the ground hard, pain sparking throughout her entire body, blinding her.

She heard shuffling, cursing and then a shot firing.

"Cicely?" Douglas said, his voice close enough for her to tell he was the one who had pushed her to the floor. The panic threading his tone gave her the strength to open her eyes.

His handsome face was contorted with worry, his concerned gaze studying her.

"Douglas."

"Oh, thank God!" He gathered her close. His body heat chased her chills away. Still she shivered. She closed her eyes and sank into the comfort of his embrace.

"Dewhurst is out cold."

She recognized the voice and opened her eyes again to find Bridgerton watching them.

"How did you get here?" she asked.

"He came with me," Douglas said. "He found me when he realized who the culprit behind the alley attack was."

She shifted her weight, sitting up slightly, and frowned. "How did you find that out and where are we?"

"Yes, Bridgerton, explain how you had the connections with the Runners to find that tidbit of information out. They found that Dewhurst owned this abandoned storage building."

He looked from Cicely to Douglas before saying, "I dabble."

Before she could ask what that meant, the sound of feet clomping down the hallway interrupted her. He turned away as men came pouring into the room. She looked up at Douglas, who studied the earl as he moved to talk to the constables.

"What was that all about?"

He shook his head. "Not a clue and I really do not care." His gaze captured hers. "You will never know the fear I felt when I found you had been abducted."

"Probably no more than I felt when you told Dewhurst to shoot you. What on earth possessed you to do that?"

"Bridgerton's plan. We had to divert his attention." He pulled away, cupping her face with his hands, then studied the gash on her head. "Does it hurt?"

She shook her head, which caused sparks of pain to radiate from her injury. Sighing, she said, "Well, just a little."

He smiled as he bent his head and brushed his lips over hers tenderly, lovingly. It was the sweetest gesture, and her nerves, already a mess, jumbled again. Tears filled her eyes at the gentleness of the kiss. When he pulled away, he studied her.

"I did not mean to make you cry, love."

"You told him you loved me."

His face blanked. "Of course."

"Of course? You have never told me."

Guilt stole over his features and he dropped his hands. "I know. But I just assumed... I know I was wrong. I realized that and was coming to tell you when Catherine told me you had been abducted."

"Catherine?"

He nodded. "She saw the whole thing and ran for help." He sighed. "But I realized, quite belatedly, that one thing you wanted, and I wanted to give it to you, share it with you."

She smiled. "Love. But that is not all I want."

His eyes narrowed. "And what else is it you want?"

The aggravated tone of his voice had her laughing. "I don't want to be told we will marry. I want to be asked."

"I did ask."

"You did not. You told."

"I..." His face flushed red. "Oh, well, you are right."

She said nothing, just continued staring at him, waiting, hoping.

"Lady Cicely, would you do me the honor of marrying me?"

Laughing she said, "Try and stop me, Your Grace." With that, she scrambled into his arms, ignoring the pain throbbing in her head, and kissed him soundly on the lips. The conversation that had been bubbling around them dissolved.

Douglas lifted his head and found that they had gained the attention of everyone in the room. "Leave off." Then he got down to the business of kissing her back.

Epilogue

In which they live happily ever after—of course.

Douglas smiled as his wife snuggled closer to his side. The early-morning sun was peeking through a slit in the curtains, but he felt no need to rise from bed. It had been a fortnight since their wedding, and they had rarely left their bedroom. He closed his eyes as memories of last night's lovemaking washed over him. Who would have thought that this little slip of a woman would have so much energy, or could be so inventive in the bedchamber?

Then again, what more could he expect from a woman who asked him to teach her about seduction while they danced a waltz. He chuckled.

"What is that for?" She rose to stretch, completely comfortable in her nudity. She rubbed the sleep from her eyes and opened them. The drowsy, satisfied look in the depths of her chocolate brown gaze melted his heart.

"Nothing in particular." He reached out to stroke his thumb over her pert breast, focusing on her rosy nipple, smiling when it pebbled at his touch. She playfully swatted his hand away. "I was just thinking of how our life together started."

She smiled. "If I had never requested your help, you would have never noticed me."

He frowned up at her. "I do not think that is accurate, my love."

She snorted. "I guess we will never know." Her smile faded. "We need to think about returning to London."

They had run from London, wanting some peace and privacy from the excitement of a surprise wedding in society. He had tried to suggest a trip to the continent but she had not wanted to go too far from her family after the last few tumultuous weeks. It had been Cicely who had convinced him to come to Ethingham. He had not wanted the memories of his haunted past here, the sight of some of the worst of his childhood abuse, to darken his new life with her. But she had insisted on it, wanting to meet the staff. Once there, his little minx of a wife had proposed "christening" every room to rid it of its evil memories. And they'd almost accomplished that goal on this floor. He saw no reason to leave with so many rooms left on their list.

"I like it here."

She rolled her eyes, but he ignored her sarcastic look and reached out to touch her other nipple.

"You did not want to come here to begin with. Besides, Colleen wrote to say she is worried about Anna. She seems to have taken Dewhurst's duplicity to heart."

Even these weeks later, the familiar anger rose along with a fair dose of aggravation. Granted, he had saved her from the crazed man, but he should have wondered about the man's sudden interest in Anna and how solicitous he was to Cicely.

"I am just sad the State Department confiscated my diary. I know they will never tell me everything that went on." She crossed her arms beneath her breasts and pouted. "Knowing them, they will never arrest anyone. The traitors will get away with it."

"Face it. The men who did this are all dead. And it is not their crime that is the worst. While they schemed, they truly did nothing quite as horrible as Dewhurst."

She nodded. "Colleen wrote that they think he will end up in bedlam. Bridgerton had told her that Dewhurst keeps raving about deceit of the father."

She sighed again, her magnificent bosom rising then falling.

He felt his groin grow heavy as a wave of heat washed through him. Even if he lived another thousand years, he would never get enough of this woman.

"Enough of cousins and diaries and old traitors." He tugged her down onto the bed and rolled over to cover her with his body. "I thought I could convince my wife to engage in a not-so-adventurous bout of lovemaking, in of all places, a bed."

She laughed and then moaned his name as he pressed his mouth against her neck. Just before he claimed her mouth, he hesitated, his lips close to hers but not touching. She opened her eyes so they gazed at each other.

"Wife," he barked.

"Husband," she responded.

"Thank you."

She smiled. "For what, my love?"

He shook his head, nipped at her lip, sucked it. "For being so bold as to ask for lessons in the middle of a crowded dance floor. For accepting me, and especially for giving me back my hope. I love you."

She said nothing, so he drew back. Unshed tears filled her eyes.

"Oh, love, I did not mean to make you cry."

"Only tears of happiness." She slipped her hand to the back of his head and urged him closer. "Now, teacher, what are we going to work on today?"

About the Author

Born to an Air Force family at an Army hospital, Melissa has always been a little bit screwy. She was further warped by her years of watching *Monty Python* and her strange family. Her love of romance novels developed after accidentally picking up a Linda Howard book. After becoming hooked, she read close to three hundred novels in one year, deciding that romance was her true calling instead of the literary short stories and suspenses she had been writing. After many attempts, she realized that romantic comedy, or at least romance with a comedic edge, was where she was destined to be. Influences in her writing come from Nora Roberts, Jenny Cruise, Susan Andersen, Amanda Quick, Jayne Anne Krentz, Julia Quinn, Christina Dodd and Lori Foster. Since her first release in 2004, Melissa has had close to twenty short stories, novellas and novels released with six different publishers in a variety of genres and time periods. Those releases included, *The Hired Hand*, a 2005 Eppie Finalist for Contemporary Romance and *Tempting Prudence*, a 2005 CAPA finalist for short erotic romance. Her contemporary, *A Little Harmless Sex*, became an international best seller in June of 2005 in its previous novella form.

Since she was a military brat, she vowed never to marry military. Alas, Fate always has her way with mortals. Melissa's husband is an Air Force major, and together they have their own military brats, two girls, and they live wherever the military sticks them. Which, she is sure, will always involve heat and bugs only seen on the Animal Discovery Channel. In her spare time, she reads, complains about bugs, travels, cooks, reads some more, watches her DVD collections of *Arrested Development* and *Seinfeld*, and tries to convince her family that she truly is a *delicate genius*. She has yet to achieve her last goal.

She has always believed that romance and humor go hand in hand. Love can conquer all and as Mark Twain said, "Against the assault of laughter, nothing can stand." Combining the two, she hopes she gives her readers a thrilling love story, filled with chuckles along the way, and a happily ever after finish.

To learn more about Melissa, please visit http://www.melissaschroeder.net/. Send an email to Melissa at mailto:Melissa@melissaschroeder.net or join her Yahoo! group to join in the fun with other readers as well as Melissa. For chat, http://groups.yahoo.com/group/melissaschroederchat, and for news http://groups.yahoo.com/group/melissaschroedernews/.

Look for these titles

Now Available:

Grace Under Pressure

A Little Harmless Sex
The Accidental Countess
A Little Harmless Pleasure
Lessons in Seduction

Coming Soon:

The Seduction of Widow McEwan
A Little Harmless Obsession
Devil's Rise
The Spy Who Loved Her
A Little Harmless Addiction
The Last Detail

She's a princess desperate for a husband. He's a duke...or is he?

A Beautiful Surrender
© *2007 Brenda Williamson*

With her uncle poised to steal her kingdom, Princess Katerina must marry. Miraculously, a new handsome duke appears on the scene. His sexy charm makes her tingle from head to toe. But can she overlook his arrogance?

The future of Dax's country is at stake. Forced to masquerade as a duke to seduce Katerina and prevent her from marrying, he courts the princess with great success. But when someone tries to kill Katerina, his instincts are to protect the passionate lady no matter the cost.

With Dax's deception revealed and her life at risk, can Katerina still surrender her heart?

Available now in ebook and print from Samhain Publishing.

Enjoy the following excerpt...

Dax hadn't expected the princess to be beautiful. He knew nothing of Katerina when he came to Alluvia and beyond her appearance, she had an inner quality he found appealing—loneliness. He identified it well from experience. She wanted someone to cherish her for herself and not for her position or wealth. That awareness made him feel off balance dealing with her, because he wanted the very same for himself.

"Was your journey here uneventful, Your Grace?" the princess asked, not responding to his bid for a more personal acquaintance.

"Won't you even try to call me Dax?" He slipped his arm around her back and drew her against him as if they were going to dance on the sidelines of the ballroom.

"I'm sorry, Your Grace, but it would not be proper for me to address you so informally, nor is it appropriate for you to hold me this close."

He waltzed her along slower than everyone else danced, steering her farther from the view of her brother.

"Proper and appropriate are what you make of it, Princess. You appear capable of deciding for yourself what is suitable." He gave in to decorum and danced her into the crowd on the ballroom floor. "Unless you're...never mind."

The princess's soft brown eyes looked up at him with greater interest than he expected. All his information about Princess Katerina of Alluvia had, of course, been tainted by the source. She could hardly be considered a shrew or cold-hearted. Not when she gazed at him with the lustful passion of a woman willing to compromise her reputation. She spoke of them being too close, but not once did she try to remove herself from his embrace.

"Or what?" Her sweet breath fanned his face.

"Or, Your Highness, might I suggest you are uncomfortable in a man's arms?" he teased.

"I've danced in the arms of many men and I see no threat to be in yours."

"And your heart?" He pressed his hand to her back, forcing her to feel the pounding of his heart upon her breasts and discovering hers rapidly beating, too.

"What does my heart have to do with dancing?" Her eyes grew curious with a delightful sparkle, as if she were an innocent child.

"Does it always beat this fast and hard, as if trapped in a cage?"

The princess shook her head violently in several short turns. Two curls sprung free and bobbed over her left eye. Her silent protest spoke the opposite of what she wanted him to think and know about her.

Dax put a hand up and tucked the curls back into the arranged swirls. He didn't tell her how soft and silky the strands were—his attraction grew strong, like she possessed the magic to put him under a spell. He enjoyed the sensation of happiness, but now was not the right time to forget he worked toward destroying her to save his kingdom.

Wherever they went, the sea of people parted like two waves. Dax and Katerina moved carelessly between the wakes. The brightly lit room concealed nothing about the woman. She carried herself as regally as any noble. Her willowy figure intrigued him enough that he overstepped boundaries, sliding his hands wherever he pleased.

On the small of her back, he felt the heat of her body. Endowed with a healthy set of breasts on her sleek, streamlined frame, the way the princess had them cinched up in her clothing appeared to be uncomfortable. Taking note of the soft ivory swells made his cock stiff and his erection battle the cloth.

"Might I suggest some refreshments?" Dax didn't wait for her answer. He needed a drink and a reprieve from her delicious, warm body rubbing his.

From a servant passing by, he plucked two long-stemmed crystal flutes from a tray. Handing one to the princess, he took a swig from the other. Over the rim of the glass, he watched aterina's mouth part. The fine crystal touched her dusky bottom lip and she tipped the glass, gingerly sipping the wine. Her tongue peeked out and ran a slow trail over her top lip. The elegant drama enchanting him didn't end when she took another sip and the bubbles tickled her nose. She lifted a hand immediately to ward off a sneeze she didn't get to stop.

Dax put a hand to hers, holding the glass to prevent her from spilling the drink. He looked deep into her wonderful stare. A hundred places to kiss her and he thought of nowhere else than the tip of her nose. At the first chance he got, he would.

The princess shivered.

"Are you cold?" He continued holding her hand on the glass stem.

"Actually, I'm quite hot."

Her warm, wine-flavored breath caught his and tugged encouragingly at his lips. With little effort on his part, he could have her against him. From toes to nose, he wanted to meld their flesh with the thrill of passion.

"That doesn't seem hard to imagine with all the people in this room generating body heat." He envisioned his tongue thrusting between her slightly parted, plum-tinted lips, tasting the wine the way she had.

Dax discarded his fluted crystal on the credenza next to him. Then, right as her eyes blinked, he put a hand on her hip and one between her shoulder blades. The princess slid her foot closer. Her thigh brushed his and her breasts pressed against his chest. The pearlescent skin rose above the edge of her violet gown. He recognized her perfume as an infusion of rose petal water—a scent he never appreciated until now. Something else had been added. After another deep inhale, he suspected it was the natural fragrance of her sex.

Katerina's hips shifted and he moved his leg, accommodating her fit and sensing a preclimactic tension. He forced his knee against her gown, into the juncture of her thighs. She took a deeper breath. Her glassy gaze held a blend of trepidation and confusion. His stance blocked her from public view. Though not enough to prevent a passerby from seeing their closeness—tightening, aligning and fitting together as only lovers should.

The tragedy of Katerina letting the duke kiss her would be, she'd love it. She'd adore the moment, the man and the sensations of being a woman. Then he'd abandon her. She didn't know much about men, even with her brother's antics giving her insight as to what they were like. He showed sweet devotion to one and then another without ever realizing the consequences to the woman.

Katerina looked into the devil's blue eyes. Each time his fingers moved, she repositioned. Every time his body twisted, she turned to fit. The pores in her skin dampened and she shivered again. Expectation and desire held her back from the boldness of begging him to kiss her.

"We're too close."

"I know." He had his hands in all the wrong places for public appearance.

"You should move away."

"Or you could."

She looked at his naturally tanned skin and the hint of whiskers peppering his jaw. His eyebrows were combed flat and his teeth resembled polished chips of white marble. Only someone so near might notice the hair in his nose was clipped. Yet, she didn't want anyone else to be as she was, where his ιps might touch hers or their lashes fold together. Fantasies rose high in her mind. For once she didn't force them away.

The duke's hand squeezed her bottom and she heard an embarrassing moan escape her throat. As if testing her voice, he kneaded the quivering cheek of her ass again, pulling and forcing her tighter into his crotch.

His other hand slipped up her back. Scorching fingers folded around the nape of her neck and held her head firmly. She couldn't begin to think where she should put her hands.

"If I don't move, what will you do?" Her body went through a series of titillating sensations in response to the heat between them.

GET IT NOW

MyBookStoreAndMore.com

GREAT EBOOKS, GREAT DEALS . . . AND MORE!

Don't wait to run to the bookstore down the street, or
waste time shopping online at one of the "big boys." Now,
all your favorite Samhain authors are all in one place—at
MyBookStoreAndMore.com. Stop by today and discover
great deals on Samhain—and a whole lot more!

Samhain
Publishing, Ltd

WWW.SAMHAINPUBLISHING.COM